Jared's life hadn't been perfect. Meg knew how tough it was to be a single parent.

Her heart went out to him as the top of a blond head popped into sight. A cowlick so like her Luke's was sticking straight up. Suddenly, there was her son dressed in his little black jacket and T-shirt.

"Cake!" He unwrapped his hand from Jared's.

What was Jared doing with her son? She looked over her shoulder and there was Luke, eating cake.

What was going on? She looked at her son and then at the little boy she'd thought was her son, and back again.

How come this little boy had Luke's face?

* * *

Books by Jillian Hart

Love Inspired

Heaven Sent #143
*His Hometown Girl #180
A Love Worth Waiting For #203
Heaven Knows #212
*The Sweetest Gift #243
*Heart and Soul #251
*Almost Heaven #260
*Holiday Homecoming #272
*Sweet Blessings #295
For the Twins' Sake #308

*The McKaslin Clan

JILLIAN HART

makes her home in Washington State, where she has lived most of her life. When Jillian is not hard at work on her next story, she loves to read, go to lunch with her friends and spend quiet evenings with her family.

JILLIAN HART
For the Twins' Sake

Steeple
Hill®

Published by Steeple Hill Books™

Special thanks and acknowledgment are given to Jillian Hart for her contribution to the TINY BLESSINGS series.

STEEPLE HILL BOOKS

Steeple Hill®

ISBN 0-373-87318-2

FOR THE TWINS' SAKE

Copyright © 2005 by Steeple Hill Books, Fribourg Switzerland

www.SteepleHill.com

Printed in U.S.A.

He will never let me stumble, slip or fall.
For He is always watching, never sleeping.
—*Psalms* 121:3-4

CAST OF CHARACTERS

Chance—From either the French or a variation of the English Chauncy, this name means "fortune, luck."

Jared—From the Hebrew, meaning "descending." A pre-flood biblical name related to Jordan.

Luke—From the Greek, meaning "light giving." Luke was a first-century Christian who wrote one of the four Gospel accounts of the life of Christ and the book of Acts. He was known as the beloved physician.

Meg—From either the Greek Margaret or the Welsh Megan/Marged, this name means "pearl."

Chapter One

"**M**a-ma!"

Her toddler's beloved voice warmed her as it always did. Meg Talbot turned from the open doors of the hotel's exquisite ballroom and stepped into the brightness of the early June evening.

Her Luke was the one goodness in her life. As painful as it was being at the celebration for the adoption agency she volunteered for—and had adopted her baby from—seeing him made the shadows on her soul slip away.

He raced toward her in the way of toddlers, a shuffling swagger, his chubby fists pumping. He was followed by one of the teenagers who volunteered at the agency to make sure he reached her safely.

Meg nodded to the girl, letting her know it was all right, and the girl turned back to the group, where teenage volunteers from the church kept the little ones happy and laughing while their parents chatted and made donations inside the crowded ballroom. Judging by Luke, the teenagers had done a very good job. He pulsed with joy and excitement as he pounded to a stop, overshot and plowed into her knees.

"Cake!" He clutched her around both legs, probably smudging her silk slacks, but what were a few smudges? His blond hair stuck straight up at the crown, a result of a stubborn cowlick and his first big boy haircut. His blue eyes glittered, and he shone brightly from within.

"Cake!" His dimples dug deep around his wide grin. His chubby hand shot straight up. "Cake, cake, cake!"

"Come here, you." She swung him around until he was giggling, lifting her spirits, as always. She put him back and he spun himself around a few times, giggling harder as he fell into her legs. He was her special gift, the very best kind, and she would always be grateful for him. The long hours she'd put in contributing to this party for the agency was the least she could do.

Because of Tiny Blessings, she was a mom.

"Let's go get us a slice of cake, okay?"

"Yeah, yeah!" His chubby hand shot up to take hers.

His fingers were sticky, but she didn't mind. As they crossed through the open French doors and into the ballroom, she kept him deftly at her side. Everywhere she looked, she saw disaster—especially the table-cloths. The tables were largely unoccupied, but set for the meal yet to be served.

With one good yank on the hem of any one of the ta-blecloths, Luke could send the expensive-looking china and crystal and silver crashing down on top of him. So she kept a close eye on him as the sound of a violin solo lilting above the hum of the gathering crowd tugged at her buried memories and hoped she wouldn't run into anyone from the church she used to attend. Everyone had heard of her divorce.

Divorce. The shame of it haunted her still.

"Hey, Meg?" A man's voice called out above the crowd, and she automatically turned.

When she spotted Gordon Bunting, she wished she'd have kept going. Gordon was a protégé of her father's, unmarried at forty and still living with his parents despite his status as a surgeon. Her mother's voice popped into her head. "He's a doctor. Why won't you date him?"

No dating. No courtship. No marriage. The black memories from her marriage pulled at her and she fought them back. The trick was to keep walking. "Gordon. I didn't know you would be attending tonight."

"Your mother mentioned you would be here without a date."

"But I have a date. My handsome son is escorting me." She kept going. The trick was to be just cold enough so Gordon would count himself lucky that she hadn't said yes to his attempts to date her.

Love only brought pain. Men were like a hurricane's force on a sandy shore, cruel and mighty, destroying everything in their path. She was still picking up the pieces of her life and of her heart in the rubble. Gordon was like Eddie. He had an important career and an ego the size of the Atlantic Ocean.

She took her place in a long line along the refreshment tables that offered all sorts of delights. Luke reached down and studied the hem of the tablecloth, then knelt to drape it over his head.

"Meg?" A deep baritone boomed, shattering her thoughts.

Gordon, what do I have to do to make you go away? You are so not a nice man. She whirled around, "Listen, I never want to see you again. Get a clue—"

Not Gordon. The man behind her was a kindly look-ing elderly gentleman who bristled at her in surprise.

"Over here," the rumbling baritone instructed to her left—on the other side of the refreshment tables.

It took her a moment to focus. There, between the enormous glistening ice sculpture of a mother holding her child and the bountiful display of sliced fruits and melons stood a tall, broad-shouldered man dressed cas-ually in a lightweight gray sweater that made his eyes so incredibly blue.

She knew those eyes. She remembered the hard an-gular mouth that was bracketed by deep dimples, al-though he wasn't smiling. His dark hair was shorter. He'd finally grown into his nose—and she hated to say it, but Jared Kierney was more handsome at thirty than he'd been as a charming, confident football jock at Chestnut Grove High. He'd been the boy she'd never known if she'd loved or detested.

She wondered that still, she realized. There was some-thing about him that grated. Probably because he'd al-ways been eager to put her in her place in high school, to outdo her, to show her how good he was. As if she cared.

She still didn't. He was a man. He was surprisingly just like Eddie, too. A dedicated churchgoer, am ambitious ca-reer man and upwardly mobile. He was probably alike in other ways, too. Her stomach coiled tight until she felt nauseous. She felt sorry for Jared Kierney's poor wife.

His face had matured so that his angular and arro-gant jaw had seasoned into what some might think was strong and solid and manly. But she didn't think so.

She still saw the teenaged boy he used to be, so sure of himself, so full of love for the Lord that he'd glowed with it. She used to admire him, and once, when they were on the school newspaper and the student council together, she'd harbored a secret crush on him. But then the old humiliation came rushing back because he'd never shown the least bit of real affection for her.

Now what? It was too late to pretend she didn't know who he was. And it was too late to avoid him. She knew what was coming—the same torture they'd gone through at their high school reunion two year ago. The comparison of one another's life, he was always trying to one-up her, and the last thing she wanted to do was to answer his questions about her life.

Not to Jared Kierney, Mr. Perfect, who surely didn't believe in divorce, either. She laid her hand on the top of Luke's head to keep him from grabbing at the tablecloth, and faced her nemesis.

It was hard to be pleasant, but she did her best. *Be nice, be cool, move on.* "Jared. Hello. I'm surprised to see you here."

"Maybe you didn't recall that I'm a newspaper reporter. *The Richmond Gazette.*"

"You managed to say that with a lot of humility. I hear you've traveled the globe, won awards, accolades and honors."

"I'm a writer. Awards don't mean all that much to me. My family, my son, those are the things that matter."

His words felt like a zing and she blushed. Okay, so her approach to send him running off wasn't working as easily as it had with Gordon. Come to think of it, it hadn't worked very well on Gordon, either. Maybe it wasn't mean enough.

She'd have to try harder. But how? His smile was still perfect. He was just so...*perfect*. There was no

other word for him. Of course his life had gone well.
She'd never forgotten their brief meeting two years before when he'd made her feel beyond inadequate. And
now all she had was failure. Except for her son.

And it was a private failure, a private anguish and no
one's business. Especially not a man who'd spent the
better part of their high school years trying to get the
best of her.

He brazened on, oblivious to the fact that she didn't
want to talk to him but was stuck in a line that wasn't
moving forward.

"I was surprised when I saw the press release you
sent to the paper. I didn't know you'd gone back to
work, but then I guess you'd have to—" He paused and
bowed his head.

Sympathy. He felt sorry for her. Meg's jaw dropped.
Her chest tightened with outrage. She supposed he still
had the perfect life with his lovely wife and a new home
in one of the prominent Richmond suburbs—yeah, she
remembered the high school reunion vividly.

"Of course you would have heard about the divorce,"
she conceded. "You'd have heard the news from your old
high school friends. Eddie talked about your Bible study."

What she didn't say was that Eddie had been a devoted servant of the Chestnut Grove Community
Church, as Jared had once been. Had Eddie's "deep
faith" fooled everyone, or just her?

Humiliation pulled her down, and it was like she
was drowning. As if water was bobbing at her chin and
then submerging her, no matter how hard she fought
against it. She instinctively lashed out, wanting him to
leave, to go away and take the sympathy lighting his
bright blue eyes with him.

Fine for him, perhaps, but she didn't need his sympathy. She was getting used to being alone. God didn't answer her prayers. Maybe He didn't answer anyone's. Ever. Everything that really mattered she had prayed earnestly for, and did it make one bit of difference in her life?

No. Prayer had not changed one thing in her life. She'd never been able to become pregnant, although the doctors hadn't been able to say why. She'd never been able to keep Eddie interested or faithful. She'd never known what a loving husband was like. Plus, her mother was as cold and distant as ever.

But that alone wasn't enough to make her stop putting her faith in God. Wherever God was, He was blind and deaf to her. When Eddie had said he wanted a divorce, that he was in love with a respiratory therapist from the hospital, her world came crashing down. This is it, she'd told God. I'll never ask for anything ever again—just please, give Eddie a change of heart. Please make him faithful and kind.

Did it work? Of course not. She'd honestly and sincerely put all of her faith on the line, and God had failed her.

A chill chased along her spine. She did not need Jared's pity. What she didn't want to admit was that as difficult as her relationship with him had been, he'd never been a bad person. No, he'd always tried to do the right thing.

She was being unfair. She was seeing every man in the world through her hurt, as if no man could be different from Eddie. When the truth was, Jared had never done anything hurtful to her. Or to anyone she'd ever known. She could only hope he'd grown up to be that same way, and not as selfish as the other ambitious men she knew. Like her father. Like her ex-husband.

"How is your wife? I remember meeting her at the reunion. She seems really nice."

Jared's face changed. Like the blue-black of a sky before a violent storm, his eyes reflected pure sorrow. "She was really nice."

"I'm glad you found someone to make you happy." If there was a happy marriage, she added, but maybe that was her heartbreak talking. Heartbreak that had felt as bleak as the look in his eyes. The thing is, he didn't look happy. "Marriage isn't so easy, is it?"

"It should be."

She avoided his gaze, but she could feel his intent, steady as a spring rain, stirring up all kinds of feelings she didn't want to acknowledge. Maybe Jared's personal life wasn't so happy after all. Maybe he knew, too, the sadness of a relationship that took everything out of a person's soul. And then demanded more.

"It was good seeing you, Meg." He moved on and away.

Their exchange left her feeling stirred up and she couldn't say why. Tension balled up so hard, she began to choke on it. She tried breathing slowly. She tried to put aside the images and concentrate. She had work to do—well, that wasn't true. She had no more work left to do here, she'd just checked in with Kelly Young, who was in charge of the adoption agency's thirty-fifth anniversary celebration, and there was nothing for her to do now but enjoy the party.

She should have gone straight home. But no, the door had been opened to the past and it was amazing how vividly and easily the pain came rolling into her soul, bringing memories of the agony of seeing Eddie's car in front of a seedy motel, the kind rented by the hour. It would be so much better if she could take a gigantic eraser to her life and obliterate every day, every minute, every memory from the last ten years.

The line moved forward and she inched along with it, bringing her closer to the beautiful tiered cake, and she felt around for Luke. He'd been against her knee a moment ago. There he was, sticking his fingers against the towering ice sculpture. She gripped his shoulder and gently brought him along with her.

Out of the corner of her eye, she could see Jared standing on the other side of the crowded ballroom, as if frozen. His gaze turned to watch her, filled with a bleakness that seemed to reach down inside her and tug at the hopelessness in her soul.

She felt a strange stirring within her, emotions and a connection she did not want to acknowledge. She never wanted to be close to another man again. Why would she, when marriage was such a sad endeavor?

She'd discovered the truth about love. It was nothing but illusions. And she would never believe in something she couldn't see and feel, to measure and touch again.

Breathe. She dragged in air that cut as it scraped down her windpipe.

"Chocolate or white?" the hotel clerk asked, his gloved hands reaching toward the generous slices of moist cake on fancy china.

"Chocolate," she said, reaching down for Luke's hand—

No Luke.

Panic exploded into her bloodstream and she glanced around. He couldn't have gone far. He was right here just a second ago. Where was he? She scanned the area and the crowd around her. He was nowhere in sight.

No, she fought panic, he had to be here. He had to be! This couldn't be happening—

Her beloved child was gone.

Chapter Two

To her relief, she spotted the edge of a familiar black tennis shoe peeping from beneath the cloth-draped serving table. In a flash, she lifted the cloth. "Out, young man. C'mon."

Her little one gazed up at her with somber eyes, so big and blue and soulful, and she hadn't thought—as exciting as getting chocolate cake would be, he had to be troubled by so many men surrounding them. Fathers with their children. Men in their thirties, as Eddie was. Eddie, the father he'd loved desperately. And still cried for at night.

Her heart broke afresh.

"My poor baby," she said, taking his tiny hand in hers and helping him out into the light. "I'm sorry," she told the server, not even looking up. "Two plates, please."

"Yes, ma'am. That sure is a nice little boy you got there."

"I think so, too." With a thank-you, she slid the plates and child so they were out of the way of others, then gathered Luke in her arms.

He went with a sigh that sounded more like a sob. She stroked his soft blond hair, wishing she could take away his pain. All she could do was kiss his brow and breathe in his baby-shampoo scent.

"Da?" He choked. "Da?"

"Oh, baby." *I know you miss your daddy so much.* She stopped with her hand in mid air to wipe away the tear spilling down his cheek. There was something off, but she couldn't put her finger on it. There was something different. The black jacket was gone, and he wore only a black polo shirt with his matching trousers.

That was strange. Had she put that shirt on him? She couldn't remember—she could have sworn she'd dressed him in a black T-shirt, so he could still pass for formal but would be comfortable enough to play in the children's area.

Goodness, that just showed how distracted she'd been. Now the gala was underway and the media was gathering around the new director. The reporters were hard to miss with their cameras and recorders. She could relax, concentrate on her son.

She straightened Luke's trousers by giving each leg a good tug on the hem—somehow, he'd gotten his clothes all twisted around. She smoothed the shirt and rubbed a smear of dirt off the side of his cheek—where on earth had that come from? Probably from something underneath the table. Little boys were professionals when it came to finding dirt.

There. He looked like the little gift he was, his round baby face sweet and adorable. Hurt filled his big blue eyes as he studied all the men surrounding them. So many fathers. He was looking for his own.

As hard as the divorce had been for her, it had shattered Luke. How could anyone turn his back on this little boy? Rage erupted and the hot molten force of it spewed up from her chest. She couldn't do anything to fix the past, it was done and over with and there was no going back, but she would never, *ever* let another man hurt her child.

"Let's go sit down and eat cake, all right?"

He nodded, so sad that not even the prospect of chocolate cake could excite him.

Her good sweet baby. She lovingly caressed the stray strands of gold off his warm forehead, full of pride and love and gratitude. She took his hand again and led him toward the ballroom's grand entrance. One of her dearest friends, Anne, was busy talking to a reporter in front of the sign that claimed, in gold calligraphy, 35 years of helping God's littlest wonders. Come celebrate with us.

Luke was unusually quiet as she settled him down at a nearby table. She cut up his cake into little bites and handed him a spoon, but he tossed the spoon aside and grabbed a gooey piece with his fingers. She opened her mouth to remind him of his manners. Hadn't they had a talk about using good manners on the drive over?

"Da-dee come?" He sniffed, and his eyes brimmed with tears.

Maybe she'd been wrong to bring him. He'd been fragile since Eddie had abandoned him. She smoothed back his hair for a second time—his cowlick was sticking straight up and it wouldn't lie flat. "Eat your cake, baby. It's chocolate, your favorite."

He didn't open his mouth wide and jam in cake and chew with delight as he always did. Instead he sighed, the saddest sound she'd heard yet, and searched the crowd.

That illustrated exactly how miserable he was.

"Daddy?" So much hope in that voice.

Maybe he thought Eddie would be here, where so many fathers paid attention to their children.

"No, I'm sorry, sweetie." She scooped up a spoonful of cake and guided it to Luke's mouth. He opened wide and took a big bite. That was more like it.

Eddie's cruel words played over and over like a CD stuck on a track. *He's not my flesh and blood, is he?* He'd sneered over the length of the cherry table in her lawyer's conference room. *You can pretend all you want, but that squalling brat is no son of mine.*

Shock had left her speechless and her mouth hung open as she'd stared at him. As if he'd said nothing out of the ordinary, his attorney went on to discuss the division of the wedding china—Eddie hadn't wanted that, either. But he seemed to give it more consideration than the precious son who now gave a quivering sigh. At least he was eating, although not with his usual energy.

How could she fix her son's grief? Helpless, she eased down beside him.

"Da-da?"

She shook her head. He sighed again and leaned against her side. She held him and hoped the saying was true—that time would heal this wound. Luke was just a little boy. He didn't deserve to hurt like this.

Meg Kramer—no, Talbot. Jared would never get used to her married name and how ironic was it that she'd become a different person along with that name? He recognized nothing of the fiery girl who'd aggravated him through high school, although her creamy complexion and delicate features, her soft blue eyes and sassy red hair remained the same. So did the lithe way she moved, a cross between a ballerina and a high jumper.

In school, she always outdid him…when he wasn't nudging past her for the top grade on the chem test or the single vote to break the tie for senior class president.

The Meg Kramer he used to know was gone and buried.

Meg Talbot more closely resembled her mother, Sue Ellen Kramer, devoted doctor's wife and charity worker, a member of the Chestnut Grove Country Club, the Literary Club and even held a seat on the hospital board, or so rumor had it. Meg Talbot had straightened some of the curl out of her bouncing autumn locks, so they waved and rippled against her shoulders like water. All the life had drained from her aquamarine gaze.

Her chilly tone more closely resembled her mother's, too, and that was a shame. He tried to forgive her those horrible words she'd said—it wasn't personal. How could it be? The last time he'd seen her since the podium on graduation day was at the ten-year reunion, right before his life had crumbled.

He'd heard news of Meg over time, of course. He still kept a subscription to the *Chestnut Grove Herald,* and his ties to the community remained strong. He met his boyhood buddies for Bible study three Wednesday nights a month. And if his friends failed to tell him of all the local news, his mother considered it her duty. Mom had always mourned the fact that he and Meg had never dated.

His mother didn't understand. How could she? She loved her soap operas, her inspirational romances, her reruns on the old sitcom channel and her black-and-white movies. She didn't understand why a boy from the poor side of town who worked two jobs and fell asleep in junior year social studies, because it was after lunch and he was running on three hours of sleep, had no real chance with a top surgeon's daughter.

Jared had always lived in the real world. Dr. Kramer had warned him off once, and while he had a crush on Meg throughout high school, maybe had even loved her, he knew her father was right. Meg deserved the best and the best wasn't a boy who worked delivering pizzas four nights a week and at the mill on weekends.

But had the best been Eddie Talbot? Jared had heard about the divorce but little else. The experience had taken its toll, for Meg's pale blue eyes reflected dark, like a lake on a rainy day. Her mouth couldn't have known a real smile in years.

And her spirit—gone was the girl who'd loved life and the Lord. The woman who'd callously spoken to him had no joy. Only sadness.

Her words cut deep, even as he tried not to blame her. His faith taught to turn the other cheek. It was not always easy.

"I hope you've brought chocolate slices for both of us." His favorite lady on this good earth gave him a twinkling smile, even if one half of her lovely face was slightly lax from last year's stroke.

"Of course I have chocolate," he quipped. "Only the best for my mom."

"Oh, you are a good man." Her eyes misted, as she'd done often since her illness. She leaned heavily on her stout cane, as she eased into a chair beside his little son. "Someone is very excited.

"Cake." He grinned his darling grin. "Cake! Cake!"

"Wow, very good, son. And so loud, too." That was

sure a change. Chance seemed to glow as he pointed into the crowd. He was sure excited. "Mama!"

"Where did he pick that up?" Mom wanted to know.

"Probably at day care. Most of the other children his age have mothers who come pick them up. He must have learned the word from them." It hurt to think of all Vanessa was missing. She was in a better place, Jared knew, as he slipped the plates onto the table.

Vanessa. Every time he grew sad from missing her, he tried to imagine the beauty of heaven. She must be filled with joy to be in such a good place.

"Mama?" Chance had no idea what he was saying. He was only repeating what others had said.

One day, he would understand. When he was old enough, Jared would tell him of how dearly Vanessa had wanted him. How greatly she loved him.

"Goodness, Jared, have you noticed he's wearing a jacket? He wasn't wearing that earlier, was he? Either that or my mind's going." His mother chuckled, always quick to laugh, always humble. "It's probably my mind going. It's been threatening to run out the door for years."

"Now that you mention it, no, that isn't his." Jared squinted at the tailored jacket that simply wasn't in his budget to have afforded. "He probably picked it up at the play area. He was there earlier. After we eat, I'll take it back there. Wait one minute, Mom. Let me cut it for you."

"Oh, I appreciate it dear. You are my thoughtful boy."

He blushed, although he wouldn't trade her mother's love for anything. He also knew how difficult it was for her to use a fork, and being self-conscious that strangers could be watching always made it more difficult for her.

There was not always a clear rhyme or reason to the turns in life that God chose for a person. Jared thought of his mom, bubbly and one hundred percent healthy until the day she'd been leveled by a stroke. He thought of his wife's sudden death and the sad life Meg Kramer Talbot must be living.

There was a greater reason, it was all a part of God's plan. Jared believed with his entire soul. It simply wasn't always the clearest thing to figure out why bad things happened to good people.

He was still wondering about a lot of things when he caught sight of Meg across the way, talking with her friend Anne Smith, who'd also gone to school with them. His spine tingled and he felt odd, as if the floor had shifted beneath his feet, although clearly it hadn't.

What was God trying to tell him? He couldn't figure it out as his son gobbled cake as if he were starving. Strange, because the kid was usually a slow eater.

"It was the wrong decision to bring him," Meg confessed to Anne, who'd just parted company with a reporter who'd been busily taking notes. Not even chocolate cake had lifted Luke's spirits. "I had hoped this might be fun for him, but there are so many men. Men remind him of Eddie."

"Poor little guy." Anne was a great lover of children, the bookkeeper for the adoption agency and rather plain, but her inner beauty always shone whenever she was around children. Part of it was the clothes she wore so she wouldn't "stand out." She laid a gentle hand on Luke's head. "Is your cake good?"

Luke gave a soulful nod, gone was his vibrant energy and his excitement over his favorite food.

Anne's face crumpled in empathy. "Meg, I see what you mean. He's too young to understand."

Miserable, Meg pushed her untouched plate aside. Her stomach had coiled into a tight ball, making hunger impossible.

Anne helped herself to a forkful of creamy icing. "Did you know Jared Kierney's here? You've got to say hi to him, after all you two went through in school."

Meg bit her tongue. Anne was a sweetheart through and through. They didn't share the same opinion about Jared, so she said the nicest thing she could honestly say. "I ran into him. I'm sure he'll give the agency some good press."

"I'll say, especially since we placed a baby boy with him, oh, about two years ago. A cute little guy, just like your Luke. Blond and blue-eyed, just a sweetie. It was touch and go in the neonatal ICU for a few weeks, but he pulled through. It was lung problems, I think." Anne's face softened as it did every time she so much as spoke of a baby. "That was not too long before his wife passed."

What? Meg felt as if something heavy had dropped right on top of her. She vibrated with the shock of it. "Passed where?"

Surely Anne didn't mean she'd *died?*

"Oh, hadn't you heard? Vanessa Kierney passed away of a brain aneurysm over a year or so ago. Poor Jared, he—"

Oh no. Meg's brain screeched to a halt. What had she said to him about his wife? Shame left her trembling. That was terrible. She'd only meant to drive him away, so he wouldn't ask about Eddie.

Anne continued on, scraping more icing off with her

fork. "It was so great to see him again. We had the nicest talk. I've got to get around and catch up with his mom. She's watching his son. I want to see how the little tyke is doing—oh, there he is."

Please, no. Meg covered her face. She couldn't face him, not after what she'd said.

Anne kept talking. "Oh, and he's with his little boy. I can't get a good look at him, but he's blond, too. Just about Luke's size. You know, I bet his son and yours are about the same age."

All Meg could envision was the shock on Jared's face. The flash of agony in his eyes. How he'd staggered as if from a blow. "I can't go over there, Anne. Oh, I've done the worst thing, I didn't know that about Jared's wife. I didn't know."

"That she died? Well, they were closer to Richmond at the time, and you were pretty busy with your new baby. Speaking of which, this is the first time I've ever seen him leave food on his plate."

"He usually eats like a baby bird with his mouth gaping open." Lovingly, Meg turned to her child. He clutched the spoon in one fist but didn't use it. And he knew how. Maybe he was feeling insecure, being constantly reminded of other fathers with their children and regressing a little. They'd been having a few problems with that.

She took the spoon from him and loaded it with a moist and rich bite of cake. Luke opened his mouth and waited while she fed him.

He was definitely having more problems with abandonment than she wanted to think about. And she wasn't all right, either. What she'd said to Jared was a perfect example. She didn't go around saying cruel things to people. She might not like Jared, but to hurt him?

No wonder he looked shattered. Regardless of Jared's integrity as a man, his pain must be great. She knew how it felt to suddenly be out of a marriage and mourning a spouse. She knew something of how Jared must be hurting. Still.

Did that kind of pain ever go away?

"What happened to Luke's jacket?" Anne's calm sensible voice interrupted Meg's thoughts.

"Oh, I guess he must have taken it off at the play area." Absently, she ran her hand over her son's head. His hair was baby-fine and silken. And it was already time for a trim. It was falling into his eyes, when it hadn't been even earlier today.

That was a little strange, but she'd once taken off Luke's brand-new shoes that had been too large in the morning, and they were tight by that evening. A sudden growth spurt. Still, it was weird.

Everything was troubling her these days. She nudged her plate toward Anne. "You might as well finish it. There's still a lot of frosting on this side."

"I'm famished. I skipped lunch and just grabbed something quick for breakfast. Not that cake is healthy—"

"But it is chocolate. Chocolate is a recommended daily requirement."

"Good point." Anne confiscated the plate.

Shame had her feeling desperate—she wanted to apologize. She felt lower than low. "This is really troubling me. I have to apologize to Jared."

"Good idea. I'll keep Luke entertained while you're gone."

"I appreciate it." Meg handed over his spoon, too, brushed a kiss along her son's warm brow and headed toward the table where Jared sat with his son and his mother.

As she circled around families gathered at tables, talking and happy, she started feeling angry. It wasn't fair—and then she stopped herself. Look what she'd become. When had she turned so unfeeling? It was harder than she'd thought to live with a broken heart. To feel sadness slowly eating her up inside, and there was nothing she could do about it.

The crackle of a microphone came from the small raised stage. Meg checked her watch—it was time for the silent auction and catered dinner to start. She recognized the agency's dynamic new director, Kelly Young, sparkling in an exquisite gown.

Then she saw a familiar profile, granite strong and James Bond good-looking—Jared. He was seated between his mother and a child on his far side, but she couldn't really see him because of Jared's wide frame.

Across the table, their gazes met. She saw the effect of her careless words. He stiffened. The smile he had for his mother faded to a straight, unexpressive line. Shadows darkened his eyes, and he looked incredibly sad.

He'd loved his wife, Meg realized with infinite remorse. If she could take back her words, she'd do it in a flash. But she knew from living all those years with Eddie that words could wound deeply. Once spoken, they could never truly be taken back.

He turned away. She'd hurt him deeply. She watched as he spoke softly to his mother and scooted her closer to the table. Then he knelt down and reached for his son on his other side. A small child who was, like Luke, not as tall as the table.

Jared's life hadn't been so perfect. He'd known loss. She knew how tough it was to be a single parent. Her heart went out to him as the top of a blond head popped into sight around Donna Kierney's chair. A cowlick so like her Luke's was sticking straight up. Suddenly, there was her Luke dressed in his little black jacket and T-shirt, animated and loud and his cherub's face smeared with chocolate.

"Cake! Ma-ma, cake!" He unwrapped his hand from Jared Kierney's.

What was Jared doing with her son? She felt an odd tingle at the base of her neck. She looked over her shoulder and there was Luke, eating cake beside Anne, using his fingers instead of the spoon.

What was going on?

Time froze. Not even her heart dared to beat. She looked at her son and then at the little boy she'd thought was her son and back again. Her mind filled with static.

How come this little boy had Luke's face?

Chapter Three

S he *had* to be seeing things, that was it. She was working too hard, putting in long hours at the ad agency and
volunteering for Tiny Blessings, in addition to being a
single mom and fitting into the new house—

Luke swaggered toward her, his mouth smeared with
frosting. "Mama! Mama!"

This was her Luke. She wasn't imagining it. His hair
was as short as it had been before. His adorable jacket
was wrinkled and streaked with frosting from where
he'd wiped his sticky fingers. He flew into her arms before she realized she was kneeling.

"Choc'lit." Excited, Luke wiggled against her, telling her as he always did of everything that happened
whenever they'd been apart.

The little boy she held was real, right? She brushed
her cheek across his brow and could feel his sweet toddler's warmth against her. He was definitely not her
imagination so she couldn't be dreaming. This was her
son, squirming in place, all constant motion. Trouble
glittered in his sweet blue eyes. This was her Luke. It

was, and so was she hallucinating? How could there be two Lukes?

That's it, I'm losing it. She'd gone completely over the edge. Call the asylum and bring a straight jacket. This was the result of too little sleep and endless stress for months on end.

"Da-dee?"

She turned toward Luke's voice, because the child in her arms hadn't spoken. It was the one who'd hopped down from his place at the table beside Anne, frosting wiped across his rosebud mouth as he swaggered across the floor. His fist grabbed her dress sleeve as he stopped to look from her to Jared Kierney. This boy had no trouble flickering in his sweet blue eyes. This boy stuck his thumb in his mouth.

Yep, I'm definitely having a nervous breakdown. It was the only thing that made sense. She stared at the both of them, as alike as two peas in a pod, identical in every way except for their clothes.

The little boy let go of her, his eyes silvered with tears. He wasn't her Luke. But she couldn't understand. She wasn't seeing double, right? How could another little boy be the splitting image of her baby?

"Chance?" called a male voice that was somehow familiar.

Meg couldn't seem to concentrate on the man coming toward them. Her brain jammed. Her synapses refused to fire. A big hulk of a man was coming down on one knee—

"Da-da!" The little boy launched himself toward Jared, who scooped the toddler up into his big strong arms.

Over Luke's soft blond hair, she met Jared's gaze.

She saw the same shock in his eyes. Read the growing confusion on his face. He released his son, watching her with fear as the toddlers stood side by side.

Identical. The cowlicks were the same. They shared the same baby-fine blond hair that stuck up in the back. Alike high foreheads. Identical blond arched brows. Both had eyelashes so long and curly, supermodels would weep in jealousy. They shared the same button nose, bow mouth and dimpled chin....

This can't be happening. How could it be? The two boys were as alike as twins.

But Luke wasn't a twin. The agency would have told her if there had been two babies, because she would have adopted them both. See? That proved there was a mistake. This absolutely had to be a coincidence.

"Meg." Jared choked on her name. "Uh…did you adopt?"

"That's why we're here tonight." She remembered what Anne had told her. "Did you adopt from Tiny Blessings, too?"

He didn't answer; he didn't need to. The way he hugged his son in his arms, tucking the boy beneath his strong chin and holding on tight was a clear answer. Jared closed his eyes, and she wondered if he was praying.

Prayer sounded like a good idea, if there was any use in it. Fear left her trembling. Fear that any adoptive parent had—that one day, no matter how official the papers and how legal the adoption, something would happen. There was a mistake in the paperwork or the birth parent would return and her child would be ripped from her arms.

Stories like that made primetime TV interviews and

movies of the week. It happened in other states and other towns. To other people. A terror sliced through her, making time stand still. She felt the cold prickle against the back of her neck and she knew this was another turning point in her life, as certain as the afternoon when she'd been driving home after lunching with Anne and saw Eddie's car parked at a seedy motel.

Life would never be the same. She wanted to deny the boys looked alike at all, to seize her son and take him home and keep him safe. She loved him. He was her heart, everything that mattered to her.

Apparently done with his prayer, Jared opened his eyes. Pain lived there, as deep as her own. He cleared his throat. "I know what you're thinking, Meg—"

"How do you know? You can't read my mind. This is clearly some mistake. There's a reason they look so similar. They could be, well, related, like cousins are. My cousin and I look more alike than my sister and I ever could. Maybe that's it."

"Maybe. That's gotta be it." Relief chased away those worry lines on his face—but not completely. "Look, there's an easy way to settle this. Chance was born on July twenty-seventh."

Everything inside her silenced. Time screeched to a terrifying halt. She knew that if she took her next breath, then time would start ticking onward. She'd have to deal with this. She'd have to face the unthinkable that haunted adoptive parents. *What if? What if I lose him? What if there was something wrong with the adoption papers?* The what-ifs went on forever.

"That's Luke's birthday," she confessed quietly.

Jared remained motionless. They stared at the boys who turned to face each other. Identical profiles. The exact sloping little nose. The same expressions as Luke shrieked in some form of toddler greeting, and Chance watched him with thoughtful eyes before poking his thumb back into his mouth.

In the background Kelly Young was thanking the businesses that had donated goods and services for the gala and for the silent auction. "Because of your generosity through the years, we have been able to give the neediest of God's children loving families and a safe environment in which to grow. We are truly thankful and very blessed to have all of you here tonight."

Kelly's words seemed very far away, as if they were in the next state instead. Or, Meg realized, it was simply hard to hear anything over the sudden galloping thump of her pulse. Time began ticking again.

"Oh, my!" Donna Kierney must have gotten out of the chair all on her own power, because there she was, mouth agape, clutching her cane and staring at the little boys who were looking at one another as if trying to decide what to do.

"I can't believe this." Anne joined the circle. "There has to be some mistake. I don't understand."

Wordless, Meg couldn't seem to move.

"Why, anyone with eyes can see it." Donna said the fateful words, the ones that would change everything. "They're exactly alike. Those boys are twins."

Jared Kierney hadn't felt this shaky since the day the doctors rushed Vanessa away on the gurney leaving him standing in the rain in the strobe of the ambulance's siren. He'd known by the sinking of his heart that he would never see his beloved wife alive again.

He'd waited in the small waiting room for the families

of patients in surgery with the pleasant nurse offering coffee to the silent men and women, old and young, in the room. The padded couches and chairs and the serene watercolors on the flat beige walls were meant to be comforting.

But there was no comfort. He'd known the exact moment when Vanessa had slipped away—he could no longer feel her in his heart. Their bond was broken and he covered his face with his hands, asking the Good Father to welcome her home even as he wept.

The surgeon who'd come to deliver the terrible news looked haggard. They'd done everything, the doctor had assured him. Everything. They tried so hard, but the aneurysm was massive and there'd been no saving her.

He'd collapsed in grief. The hospital chaplain stayed with him until the Reverend Fraser made it in through the near hurricane conditions. As the storm battered the stout walls of the hospital, Jared had grown calm. This was God's decision. Vanessa's brain damage would have left her unable to hold their baby son. Years of physical therapy would have made little difference.

So it was merciful, he understood, that God had taken Vanessa from her broken body. And given her a perfect and happy place in Heaven.

Jared was grateful. While he feared for that horrible first month after the funeral that he might not survive his grief, it was only the agony of a husband missing his wife who'd been his match in every way. That was all. He was hurting, but Vanessa was not.

During the long nights, when he could not fall asleep in their bed without her, he would be aching for her with all of his being. He would remember what the doctor had said to him. "If she'd lived, she would have suffered terribly. She would not have been able to speak or to move. She may never have come out of the coma. God was merciful. Be thankful, for her sake."

That's what true love was—wanting the very best for the other, not for yourself.

And so it was with a greater love he'd stumbled through his day and did his best to father their precious child. Managed to work and pay the mortgage and rock his son to sleep every night. And he felt, with the whisper of a breeze through the opened window or the hush of moonlight at night, that she was watching over them. That her love remained—a protective light, somehow, from above.

And Jared had given extra thanks for their son. Chance, awaited for so long, was the gift that had gotten him through. That had kept him breathing and walking and living.

Love, pure and fierce, choked him as he stared at the two boys in front of him.

This couldn't be right. There had to be a reasonable explanation. He cleared the panic out of his throat, but his breath sounded choked as he watched Chance take a bite of the chocolate cake. Frosting smeared his fist and transferred onto his face. Then he grinned.

Jared lost his heart, as he always did, every time his son smiled. He was grateful to Mom and to Anne Smith for taking the boys to sit at the table and keep them occupied with more pieces of cake, so he and Meg had the chance to try to deal with this.

Deal with it? How was he going to do that? He had a hard time trying to wrap his mind around it. His heart didn't want to acknowledge what his eyes witnessed, even if it was obvious his mother was right. She watched over the two boys as they played with their cake, and both were pocked with spots of frosting and chocolate crumbs. Identical creases of thought dug into their high foreheads as they both stared at their sticky hands and, as if a mirrored image, dipped their blond heads in the same way and licked the frosting off their fingers.

"Those are not good manners, young man." Meg wasn't stern, and that surprised him. The woman he saw before him was gentle, and he saw in her a hint of the girl she'd once been.

"Uh-oh." Her Luke held up his sticky hands, in the same way his son did and gave an innocent shrug as if he simply couldn't help himself. Big shining blue eyes sparkled with innocence.

Just like Chance.

Twins. He'd hunt down the truth, he wasn't an award-winning reporter for nothing. Contacting Kelly was first on his list for Monday morning, but he knew what he would find. He felt it with the iron-solid certainty that had served him so well in his work and in his faith. He already knew the answer, because he felt it in his heart.

As for Meg, she'd hitched her chin higher and turned to her child. Apparently she wasn't ready to talk yet, so he waited while she extracted a wet wipe from her well-organized diaper bag and began to scrub clean her son's hands. Silvered tears stood, but did not fall as she worked.

Jared could see inside her at that moment—he didn't know how or why. He saw a woman whose spirit was drowning in pain. He felt the agony her ex-husband had put her through. He read the fear of losing custody of her son and recognized a love so pure and bright for her little boy. Jared realized, too, that God had given Luke to Meg so that she would survive her husband's cruelty.

The same way he had been given Chance, to help him through the grief of losing Vanessa. To give him a new life to build from the pieces of the old.

Jared felt the tingling deep within his spirit, whenever he was aware of God working in his life. His memory verse from Sunday school rang in his mind. "The Lord says, 'I will guide you along the best pathway for your life. I will advise you and watch over you.'"

He was a deeply faithful man. He trusted the Lord and worked hard to be a good servant. But it was not easy to gaze upon his son and Meg's and trust that no bad would come from this. No harm. He knew God worked for the good of those who loved Him.

It was only human to want to grab up his small and vulnerable son, to protect his innocent spirit and take him as far away from Meg Kramer Talbot as he could get.

But that was not right. It was not what the Lord would expect him to do.

So he made his shoes take him forward until he was standing beside Meg. Behind the chairs where the twins sat side by side. "Would you mind if I asked for one of those wipes?"

"Sure." As if afraid to look at him, maybe for what she might see, she stiffly knelt to snap a fresh wipe out of a container. Woodenly she offered it to him.

Jared could feel his mom's questioning gaze, but he trusted they would find time to talk about Chance's brother later. What mattered right now was helping Meg cope with this. They would have to help one another, he figured as he washed his son's sticky face and hands.

Please help me find the right words, Lord. He could sense Meg's fear. He was afraid, too, but he knew that what happened next for all of them, whether it was a battle or a good outcome, depended on how he acted at this exact moment.

He waited until Meg was done cleansing her son, who was bouncing around on his chair, squirming with endless little-boy energy.

"We need to talk. Mom will watch them," he reassured her.

"Luke is so fast. I can barely catch up with him if he gets a good head start."

It wasn't what she was worried about, but he understood she needed reassurance. "Look, Anne is sitting down next to them. They'll be all right while we step outside."

She paled. "I don't want to talk."

"I know."

Applause shattered the relative stillness in the ballroom. Gerald Morrow, Chestnut Grove's influential mayor, took center stage and smiled benevolently at the crowd gathered beneath him. Seeing the mayor reminded Jared that he wanted to get a short interview for the piece he was writing on the gala.

But information gathering took second place as he felt a child's hand grab his shirtsleeve and tug. It was Luke, with hurt blue eyes. It was a mind-reeling experience to look at the boy who was exactly like his son, but wasn't. He was an entirely different child, and yet that knowledge didn't stop his heart from jolting.

Luke's bottom lip trembled. "Da-dee. Bye. No more."

He held up his hands to show there was nothing in them. Big silver tears filled Luke's eyes and dripped downward without a sound.

Tenderness ached within him for this boy he did not know. And felt that he did. He had no right, but he reached without thinking to thumb away those tears. He felt the boy's hurt. Read him as easily as he did his son.

"Luke!" Meg snatched up her child, kissed the tracks where his tears had been.

Like the old days, he thought, seeing the emotions whirl through her as he could when they'd been high school kids. He'd never been able to see inside someone so clearly, not even Vanessa—and after seven years of marriage he'd never been able to interpret her moods.

But Meg—he could feel the wrenching need to protect, the hurt and the anger. While she settled the diaper-bag strap on her shoulder and kissed her son's forehead, he saw the love in her, sweet as spring blossoms. All this he felt, but watching her, he could only see the polished way her soft red hair shone in the faint lights.

Maybe it was just his reporter's instincts doing overtime—or his imagination getting away from him. The last thing cool-and-collected Meg Talbot looked to be was emotionally charged. Reserved, composed, her chin was up and her slim back was straight.

Cold words, quietly spoken but they held the punch of an arctic freeze. "I'll thank you not to touch my son."

Just like that, the princess had dismissed the lesser peasant. It still rankled that she could make him feel that way when he knew good and well it wasn't her intention. She was simply imperious—it was who she was, who she'd been raised to be and the only problem was that it still hurt.

She spun on those high heels, tapping away through the crowd. The mayor's speech knelled from the speakers overhead, and the crowd chuckled and applauded as she did her best to escape him.

He scooped up Chance, tucked him safely against himself and followed her through the throng. Folks called out to him, people he knew, but he kept going, promising to come back. By the time he reached the revolving entry doors, Meg was nowhere in sight.

He knew why she was scared. Why she'd panicked when she saw him try to comfort her son. Adoptive parents lost their children—it happened. Meg loved her son. She would break if she lost him.

Jared knew, because that's the way he felt about Chance. Although he didn't like Meg Talbot, especially the shell of a woman she'd become, he wanted to find her and reassure her. Where had she gone?

He spotted her outside along the gracious curving drive where shuttle buses unloaded passengers and valets and baggage boys hurried to do their work. She balanced her son on her hip, clutching him with both hands, mother and child nearly hidden beneath the shade of a reaching magnolia tree. The low sun shot blinding rays through the branches and he lost sight of her as a blue minivan pulled up to the curb.

He started hurrying, but it was too late. By the time he'd fought his way around carts of luggage and hordes of tourists and late-arriving guests to the celebration, the spotless blue minivan was cruising away. Red taillights flashed as she slowed for the light change at the intersection.

How could she run off like this? What about the boys? He'd handled it badly, he realized. Of course a woman who'd nearly been broken in a bitter divorce and custody battle would be terrified at the prospect of bringing into question anything about her son's adoption.

Jared wished he could hit Rewind and replay the last few minutes.

"Mr. Kierney? Please, tell me you are not leaving already!"

The woman's voice penetrated his thoughts. He recognized Lindsay Morrow, the mayor's wife, clipping toward him as quickly as her designer spike heels and her narrow expensive skirt would allow. "You gave your word to write up a substantial piece on Gerald for your paper. Are you aware by standing out here you are missing his speech?"

"Yeah, I'll be right in."

When he looked next, Meg had vanished in the glare of the setting sun.

Jared couldn't forget the pain on Meg's face. That one moment when surprise had stripped her bare and he'd seen into her heart.

Oh, Meg, what did he do to you? His chest constricted with hurt for her. For the Meg Kramer Talbot he'd seen in that instant was not the Meg he'd ever known. He still didn't know how to interpret what he'd seen, and it was more than his journalist's instinct telling him there was more to know about this woman he'd tried not to care for through his high school years.

Even more, with years and miles and marriages between them, he still wanted to care. He'd almost been fooled by her competent and capable facade. The I-don't-need-anyone strength to her that didn't match up with what he'd glimpsed within her.

She'd radiated so much pain.

Newly divorced, it didn't take a genius to figure out why she was hurting. He wondered what the man who'd vowed before God to honor and cherish her had done to fail her.

She hadn't been the only one on his mind tonight, making the brilliant evening of celebration seem like background noise. The mayor was in the center of the room, with his lovely wife on his arm, still talking to a circle of some of the wealthiest citizens of Chestnut Grove. And Kelly's genuine enthusiasm and belief in her work at the agency sparkled like the crystal facets of the overhead chandeliers.

As worthy as this event was, it was the reason he had his son. His son that was the identical twin of Meg Talbot's.

They had to be twins. He didn't want to admit it, but he knew that it was true. He needed to find out what had happened, why the agency had separated the boys without telling either adoptive couple—well, the agency would be closed, and as badly as he wanted answers, this wasn't the place.

There were more important concerns. Like Chance. Jared put away his things, but his entire focus was on the boy snoozing contentedly in his grandmother's arms. Innocent and good-hearted, with his cowlick twisted up and his precious face relaxed as he slept.

Pure love beat within him, and he'd do anything to protect his boy. Do anything to keep him safe and happy.

And so would Meg Talbot, for her little boy. He

zipped the leather case, and unloosened his tie. The festivities were over, the hotel staff were beginning to clear the tables that had emptied and the clink and clatter of fine china and silver rang pleasantly against the drone of voices from the guests still talking.

He was ready to call it a night. What he needed was to get home, get Chance settled down and spend some time alone. Sorting through all this before Monday morning rolled around and he had a plane to catch.

What am I gonna do about that? His stomach fisted as he thought about the demands of his job. His editor was pressuring him, the higher-ups were waiting to see if he had what it took, and now…

Chance has a brother. Jared circled around the table, avoiding his mom's knowing eyes, and came up beside his sleeping son. He whipped off his tie and jammed it into the jacket's pocket before he knelt. His chest was a painful mix of emotions he couldn't begin to wrestle down, but when he gazed upon his boy the troubles faded away.

All that mattered, all that would ever matter, was this child.

Love and pride warred for first place within him as he gathered Chance in his arms. Holding him sure and tight, Jared wished he could always be strong enough to protect his son from the heartaches of the world. *What happened that you are all by yourself, little boy?* The questions haunted Jared as he grabbed his bag and his mom's enormous purse.

She was already on her feet, her face serene as if she was not worried. His mother was one amazing woman.

Unbowed by her hardships, she took a halting step. "I don't know when I've had such a lovely time. To think, the agency raised so very much money."

"It was a fine success," he agreed, absently. He couldn't help it. He couldn't seem to focus his thoughts. They kept running away from him.

Meg must be like this, too, thinking in circles. What if? What would happen? What if the boys shouldn't have been separated?

And now that they knew, even if the adoptions were fine and legal and separating the children had been a wish of the birth mother, then what did they do now?

Lord, I hope You're watching all that's going on down here tonight, because I could really use some guidance. Jared felt a punch down deep. Certain that he and his family were in the Lord's capable and loving hands, he kept even with his mom's slower pace and added one more request for God: to watch over Meg Talbot, who seemed so lost.

Chapter Four

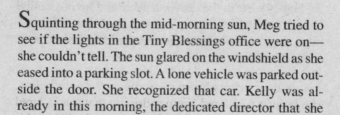

Squinting through the mid-morning sun, Meg tried to see if the lights in the Tiny Blessings office were on—she couldn't tell. The sun glared on the windshield as she eased into a parking slot. A lone vehicle was parked outside the door. She recognized that car. Kelly was already in this morning, the dedicated director that she was.

That's a good sign. Meg tried to soothe the fears that had kept her wide-awake all night, but until she heard that her son's adoption was not compromised, nothing was going to quiet this roiling sickness in her stomach. She pulled into the first spot she came to, killed the engine and grabbed her bag.

This was the moment of truth. Pulse pounding, she took one last look at her son. She could see him in the rearview mirror, tucked safely in his car seat and singing, although the overhead video screen had switched off with the engine. That didn't seem to trouble her son at all. He clapped his hands and hummed, and swung his feet against the seat.

Love so pure and strong burned through the bleak pain in her heart. It seemed to be the only thing she could feel these days, but she didn't mind. He was what mattered. She joined in the song as she climbed out into the humid morning and unbuckled him from his car seat. His arms reached around her neck and held tight as she transferred his weight onto her hip. Her soul went all soft and glowing. *I cannot lose you, little boy.*

She hiked the bag on her free shoulder and hit the remote to shut the side door and then lock it up when she heard the rasp of tires on the pavement behind her. As she moved into the shade of the building, she noticed a gleaming navy blue truck, sleek and masculine, pull into the lot behind her.

A strange feeling skidded down her spine. She couldn't see through the glare and the tinted windshield, but she could feel him. She didn't know how or why, but without being able to see through the tinted glass, she *knew* it was Jared Kierney driving that truck, Jared Kierney who was watching her as he parked his vehicle beside hers.

The door whispered open and Jared appeared. The sunlight seemed to worship him as always. The wind ruffled through his thick dark locks like an old friend. "Hey, Meg. I shouldn't be surprised you're here, too. This is great. We can go in together."

"I'm not sure I need you to help me handle this." She didn't mean to sound snotty, it just came out that way. Everything came out wrong when she was around Jared— at least *that* hadn't changed since their high school days.

"Well, I'll just wait out in the reception area until you're done explaining about your boy's look-alike." He winked, not at all offended.

He ought to be offended. What annoyed her the most about Jared Kierney was his undefeatable good mood. How he seemed to see the bright side of everything, the good in everybody. He went to church every Sunday, led a Bible study group and played golf with the minister. And unlike her ex-husband, he was sincere about it.

Then he opened the second door to the extended cab and to her surprise lifted out his little boy. His hair was tousled and he was sucking his thumb. It was like looking at her Luke. Her mind simply could not get used to looking at the two of them.

Jared slammed the door, swung his son into the crook of his arm and joined her at the front door. "I know what you're thinking. You thought my mom would have him."

"I assumed she must be taking care of him."

"A lot of people thought after Vanessa died, I'd hand Chance over to my mom to raise. Or get remarried right away, so I'd have someone to take care of him. He was only two months old when we lost her." He reached around her and snatched the door out of her hands, holding the heavy door for her whether she liked it or not.

She didn't like it, but she stepped through it. Jared really was a kind man. "I am sorry. About you losing your wife and Chance his mother. And about how I was a jerk about it last night. I truly didn't know or I never would have said such a thing."

"I know." His gaze raked hers, and it was no ordinary look. It was like a touch to her soul. She felt too revealed and shivered, turning away, but as she walked into the agency, it felt as if they were still gaze to gaze. As if there was some kind of an emotional connection or awareness…she didn't know what it was. Only that she had glimpsed into his heart, just as he'd seen into hers.

Sadness. That's what she'd sensed deep within him. He'd lost his wife. He'd lost his love and the dream of a future with Vanessa. Although divorce was not the same as losing a partner to death, it was a death in a way—of a dream, of a marriage, of a commitment to another person.

She'd lost enough recently to have some idea of the great sorrow in Jared's soul. It changed how she saw him, the confident steady manner of his didn't seem superficial, it was more like strength.

"Meg!" Kelly greeted, strolling around the corner. "I can't thank you enough. Last night was a great success and if you hadn't arranged—"

She stopped mid-sentence, her attention riveted on the second little boy as Jared moved into her line of sight. Kelly looked from Luke to Chance, and Meg could read the progression of thoughts from how close they looked, to no, they really looked alike, to no, they *are* alike.

Jared broke the stunned silence, calm and easygoing as always. He held Chance close. "Meg and I discovered this, uh, similarity at the gala and we'd both like to know exactly how likely is it that we have a problem with the boys' adoptions."

"I'm guessing Jared didn't want to involve an attorney, like I don't, unless it's necessary. Maybe there's just some kind of an explanation." Meg couldn't imagine what, but she wanted her son's adoption to stand uncontested. She fervently wished that there was a perfect explanation. And, without that, that whatever the truth was, she would not lose her baby.

"Why don't you come on back?" Kelly looked rattled, but only for a moment longer. She was professional and as polished as could be, and a good person at heart. "Go ahead and take a seat at my desk. I'll just see if I can't pull the boys' files. Did you two want any coffee or tea?"

"No, thanks," she and Jared said in unison.

Kelly snapped efficiently out of sight, and Meg, knowing the way since she volunteered here from time to time, headed deeper into the office. Jared said nothing, either, but he, too, kept a close look on his boy, as if he were afraid he might lose him.

It was strange they had this in common. They'd lived such different lives since high school. They'd gone to different colleges, found different jobs, and she'd seen him only once in twelve years until yesterday, when in high school she'd seen him every day. Every day as they worked on the yearbook and the school newspaper, and in the advanced college-placement classes. Everywhere she used to turn, there was Jared.

Maybe, she realized now, she hadn't minded seeing him so much. Maybe her real problem with him had been, if she admitted the truth, that the reason she'd disliked him so much was that he hadn't seemed to care for her as much as she'd secretly cared for him. And now they were here, in the same situation, desperately hoping that Kelly was going to tell them they were imagining an undeniable likeness. And that there was no reason to worry either of them might lose their child.

After some time, Kelly marched into sight, and Jared drew away and retreated to a safe distance. They both watched in anxious silence as she circled around to her desk. There was a streak of dust smeared across the cuff of her tailored slacks, but she had two file folders in hand. The furrow of worry cut deep into her forehead told Meg there was no good news.

"I'm afraid there's not a lot of information." Kelly looked truly sorry. "What I did find is troubling."

Meg's last hopes fell. She felt Jared's hand on her shoulder. It was a sustaining touch, meant to comfort her. When she looked up at his handsome face, set as if ready for the worst of all possible verdicts, her defenses against him melted a little. At least they were in this together. He was a good man. His heart was in his eyes. His love for his son shone so bright and strong, it was hard to see anything else.

Feeling a similar love, and a similar anguish, Meg held her son more tightly.

"The boys are twins. There is no doubt about it, not that it isn't obvious when you see them together." Sympathy softened Kelly's face. "It seems that Luke was the healthier of the two, and he was adopted right away. But Chance was a little underweight and had a problem with immature lungs, so he was kept in the hospital for several months. He should have been placed with you, Meg, not with Jared."

There was no way to describe her relief, but she felt Jared's shocked silence, and she knew what he was thinking. That by rights, he never should have had Chance and now there was no way he could stand to give him up. It would be like ripping out a part of his soul.

"What does this mean for the adoptions?" she asked, because it looked as if Jared couldn't.

"We'll have to examine this all more carefully. I suggest getting lawyers if you want to. I guess the question is for you, Meg, you should have received both boys. Is that something you want to pursue?"

"To take Jared's son from him? No!" Horrified, she sank into the closest chair. Luke was getting heavy so she let him down; he'd been squirming anyway. He dropped to his knees and looked at Kelly from beneath the bottom edge of her desk. Chance struggled to get down and squatted down next to him. Both blond cuties waited quietly for Kelly to notice them.

She shot them a surprised look, although she'd noticed them all along, which made Luke squeal and Chance smile.

Meg noticed that Jared still hadn't said anything. He had to be devastated. He couldn't seem to take his eyes off his son.

Kelly broke the uneasy quiet. "I am sorry about this. It's no excuse, but this isn't the only problem I've found in the records since I took over. I wish I could say there was an easy solution to your problem, but there isn't. I'm here to help in whatever way I can."

Jared nodded and cleared the emotion from his throat. Whatever he'd come here to discover, it hadn't been this. He wanted reassurance. He figured the adoption papers were signed, sealed and recorded long ago. Chance was his son. His life. His world. He'd already lost Vanessa, and if he had to give up his child now…

Don't think about it, man. He would stay calm, call his attorney and believe. He wasn't alone. God was on his side, and this would work out. He had to believe it.

"I don't have any questions right now." He caught Chance up in his arms and it was his turn to walk away.

The questions Meg had last night had continued to trouble her all the way home. One question had been answered. The boys were twins, but the legality of the adoption, the fact that she should have gotten Chance, troubled her the most.

How important were the birth mother's wishes on the adoption? Were they enough to cause problems now? She didn't know, and since it was a beautiful Saturday morning in June, it wasn't likely she would find her attorney taking calls. To make matters worse, her head was starting to pound.

Drink more tea, Meg. She put down her gardening tools and collapsed on the bottom step. There was a porch swing with a really comfortable cushion at the top of the steps, but she was too beat to make it that far. She stretched to reach her insulated glass and sipped the sweet iced tea. The coolness washed across her tongue and cooled her from the inside out.

Much better. Now, if she could manage to relax, maybe the tension headache would decide to go away.

A dog at the end of the block gave a single bark. Flash, the neighbor's lethargic Doberman, must have summoned up enough energy for one woof to announce the presence of either a kid racing by on a bike or Mr. Wilson, who kept eighty-two years young with a robust walk every morning in the summer before it became too hot.

She was not prepared for Chance Kierney, riding on top of his father's shoulders. Jared held him safely as he lumbered down the shade-dappled sidewalk. Her little boy, who'd been racing in circles through the sprinkler she'd set up for him while she weeded, skidded to a stop at the sight of the man and child approaching.

Jared stopped where the sidewalk met the front walkway. He opened his mouth as if to speak first, but then must have thought better of what he planned to say. He closed it again, his jaw clamping shut with a click of teeth. He was vulnerable, too.

"We're in the same boat, aren't we?" The confession slipped from her tongue, when she'd meant to keep it vaulted up inside.

"I want to say yes, but it's not true. I have more to lose than you do. I guess I need to know if you're going to pursue what Kelly told us. That Chance should have been with you."

"I will not ever take your child from you. Please, don't ever worry about that. I know what that's like. My ex-husband had threatened to take Luke, but he'd only wanted to hurt me. I didn't know that at first, and I'd never been so afraid. I couldn't do that to someone else."

"I'm pretty relieved to hear that." He lowered Chance to the ground.

"I'm more worried what this does for both adoptions. Kelly's right. It's time for a lawyer."

Across the length of front lawn, their gazes met and she saw the truth in him. Realized she could see his heart as easily as she had when they were in school. Pain tightened his face. "I have a solution, if you'd like to hear it."

"I was just about to have another cup of iced tea. Would you like some?"

"If you'd give me tea with lots of ice and let me sit on that porch of yours, I'd be grateful."

"It's been a tough day so far, hasn't it?"

"Yep. I don't think I've had anything to eat or drink yet."

"I'll see what I can do. Come sit and keep an eye on the boys for me?" Her eyebrow shot up at the question, softening it. She could see that they were in this together, and there was no easy solution.

He nodded, appreciating her understanding more than the tea.

"Uh?" Chance tipped his head back to ask.

"Go play." He nodded toward the sprinkler where Meg's little boy was standing bare chested and wearing denim shorts with a train embroidered along the cuffs. His soulful blue eyes watched every move with that toddler innocence as Chance swaggered toward the sprinkler.

Luke looked startled and took off at a run, circling around to hit the cold spray of water. A shriek of delight had Chance clapping. When Luke appeared through the spray, still running, Chance took off after him, a silent follower. He shouted in glee at the first cool blast of the sprinkler and kept on running.

Jared's heart broke at the sight because there was no denying it. It seemed unreal that suddenly his entire world could do a one-eighty, but it had happened before when he'd lost Vanessa. The identical little boys ran in single file, like a little train, in a circle around the sprinkler and then through it. Chance was shining—he was having a good time.

All I want are good things for you, little man. He studied Meg's house. The craftsman-style bungalow was painted a buff yellow with white trim and shutters. It was in good shape and a nice house—from the porch swing with colorful pillows to the wide picture windows in the living room and master bedroom, he figured. A three bedroom house. Roomy enough.

The screen door whispered open and there was Meg. The sun caught on the glass in the door and for a moment, rays of light cut through his line of sight. For a moment he saw the girl he knew in memory, bright and cheerful and rosy cheeked. Then the woman Meg had become emerged through the image as the door clicked shut and she was taller, curvy and mature. Sadness seemed to cling to her and, if he closed his eyes, he swore he could feel the devastation of heartbreak from her marriage, like rubble after an earthquake.

He didn't see how this would ever have a chance, but he had to try. He had to ask her. He took her soft smile, a non-verbal invitation to join her on the porch, as a good sign. Leaving the boys to their play, he ambled up the rest of the walkway.

The steady hiss of the sprinkler changed. Somewhere he heard it, but he was too focused on what he was going to say next.

"Jared, get back!"

He heard her too late. The first spurt of cool water splatted directly in the center of his T-shirt. The second shot him right in the face. He hopped back, noticing the sprinkler had overturned. One of the boys had accidentally knocked it with one of their feet. They both stood still with identical looks of dismay on their sweet cherub faces.

"Well, since I'm already wet." He fearlessly grabbed the sprinkler and let the cold water cool him down some as he repositioned it for the boys. "Okay?"

Luke and Chance watched him silently and nodded.

"Good. Then go!"

Sounds of glee rang in the air once again as he lumbered up the steps and onto the porch. "I'll just sit on the step. I don't want to drip all over your nice cushions."

"No, don't worry about it. Sit. I'll bring a towel." She patted one of two matching white wicker chairs before she slipped away again. A cat curled up on the porch swing slitted one eye to give him a disapproving look, as if the creature knew exactly why he'd come and was stating its opinion.

Jared looked around, considering the very feminine touches of colorful pillows on wicker furniture, flowerpots spilling blossoms and a dainty wind chime overhead tinkling in a gust of wind. She'd been weeding. Earlier she must have mowed the lawn because that fresh cut grass scent was in the air, as well as a few stray clippings drifting like dust across the cement walkway. He tried to imagine what it would be like if she said yes to his proposition.

And then he realized, why should she? She was doing just fine on her own. She'd bought a house and obviously made it a home. She was providing for her son. She had friends and family to help her. A great job at one of the best advertising firms in the state.

And then the boys' laughter lifted over the rustling leaves from the oaks lining the sidewalk and the hiss of the sprinkler and the faint bark of a dog from down the street. The sprinkler was again on its side, only this time Luke had a hold of the hose and was holding it high over his head to spray Chance full blast. Chance was giggling and wiggling in the spray.

"Look at them. I can't believe how cute they are." Meg tossed him a fluffy yellow towel that was folded precisely.

"Thanks."

He lost his breath when he looked at her. The wind lazed through her hair, stirring it softly against her soft oval face, and the rich red locks were softly curly and brushing the top line of her slim shoulders. She planted a fist on her hip, not coltish thin as she'd been in those days, but curvy and elegant even wearing the simple denim cutoffs and a faded navy T-shirt, with her bare feet shoved into navy blue sneakers.

It was hard to believe so many years had passed, rushing like water in a quick-paced current. Bringing them together again. What would have happened, he wondered, if he'd told her back then how he felt? That his secret crush on her could have been something much deeper? Would she have laughed at him? Or would she have wanted him?

He'd always feared she would have said a resounding no. Twelve long years later, here he was sitting here on her porch afraid of the same exact thing.

"You said something about having a solution?" She eased into the porch swing and the cat, who'd been emanating disapproval, leaned against her fingertips and purred. "I'd love to hear anything you have to say. I just don't want my little boy hurt by any of this."

"Exactly. I'd gladly give up anything, my life, to keep Chance safe and well." He took a sip of iced tea and seemed to be thinking. "Maybe this is a better idea than I thought. I think it might be the best possible solution. The boys look pretty happy being together, don't you think?"

Meg watched as Luke beamed. She melted inside at the wide grin and joyful sparkle to his entire little spirit as Chance tugged on the hose, wanting to hold it, too, and he let go. The boys' gazes met and locked for a long moment. Were they recognizing the other? No, they were too young to begin to understand, but as Luke let go of the hose, and stood for his brother to squirt him, there seemed to be a strange bond between the two. Without words, they seemed to communicate.

"He's never done that before. He likes to be in charge," Meg confessed. "And he's too young to understand the sharing thing."

"Did you see how they traded places? Do you think they know they're brothers?"

Brothers. It had new meaning. "The boys are family."

"And you and I aren't." He crunched on an ice cube and long moments stretched between them.

Meg saw her independent future fading away. The boys should be together somehow. Did that mean something like a shared custody arrangement, where she and Jared were always trading between having the twins and being alone without them? Did that mean she had to sell her house and move to Richmond, where Jared lived, and buy something close to his house, so the boys could see one another more often?

Too many questions tore at her. She only knew her life and Luke's were never going to be the same. This stable and secure environment she'd tried to build for him here wasn't so stable after all.

Finally Jared spoke. "What I've been thinking long and hard about is this and there's only one solution that is best for the boys. Marry me."

"What?"

"I can offer your son something he's never had—a real man for a father. A man who will love him and treasure him. I will treat him like my own. Well, he's exactly like my own already."

A deafening rush drowned out the rest of his words. Jared was talking, only she couldn't hear him. She could see his mouth moving, but it was as if she'd gone deaf. The rush was her blood pulsing through her ears and the rapid, terrified cadence of her heart. "No!"

"Wow, that was fast. I know we're not in love, but we know each other—"

That was all she could hear, the words faded away exactly as if she were a drowning person sliding beneath calm, fathomless water. Sliding down until there was no noise and only a faint beam of light and then nothing. Nothing at all.

"No, Jared. I can't do that again. I won't go through that again."

She sprang up, needing to get away. The screen door banged behind her and she realized she was in the kitchen without realizing she'd come so far into the house. She was shaking. She was panicking. *I will not marry anyone again. Ever.*

She could see him through the screen door. The boys had come up to him, dripping wet, hopping and giggling. A delighted shriek echoed through the house as he grabbed the twins, tucked one in each arm and charged down the steps. The sprinkler caught all three of them as Jared began to turn in place, gaining speed as the boys laughed and screeched.

Shared custody, that had sounded horrible a few minutes ago, but now it sounded like a good idea. Jared was a decent man. He'd raised Chance without a wife's help, and look how the little boy had prospered. He'd stayed and cared for a baby, which anyone who'd had a baby to care for knew the challenges and hard work that went hand in hand with the joys of it. The commitment. She knew few men who would have done the same. Not her father. Not Eddie.

But Jared. He was an excellent father. As he lowered the boys carefully to the ground, Luke caught him around the neck and held on so tight. Although she was too far away, and the rush in her ears made it impossible to hear, she could read the words shaping his adorable rosebud mouth.

"Da-dee."

Oh, little boy. I know you want a father. Meg leaned against the wall, feeling her life come to a dead halt. What did she do? How did she marry a man who she really didn't know?

Jared was bounding up the steps, dripping wet again, and he hauled open the door. "Are you all right?"

She nodded. His concern for her feelings was more overwhelming than his proposal had been.

"Then think about it." He was firm, but kind, and it was a dizzying combination. "I have to go out of town, but I'll be back on Saturday. Have an answer for me, okay? Either way, yes or no."

She nodded, not knowing what to say. She listened to the door swing shut and Jared's retreat. And then nothing. Nothing at all. She went outside to bring Luke in, but Jared had already turned off the hose and was coiling it up, Chance watching next to him.

Marriage. How could that be a good solution? She held out her hand for Luke and waited for him to come. He hesitated on the top step and stuck his fingers in his mouth.

"Da-dee come?"

How could she stand the hurt in her baby's eyes?

"Later," she told him and gathered him tight in her arms.

Chapter Five

Meg shouldered open the diner's glass-and-chrome door, whipped off her sunglasses and sighed at the sweet breeze of the air conditioners.

It was blazing hot already, although she wore her favorite carpenter shorts that were baggy and beyond comfortable, and a summery sweater set in daffodil yellow that always put a snap in her step. Today she needed the positive cheerfulness of the color because she was feeling anything but happy.

Disenchanted, panicked, horrified, yes. But happy? No way. She did not want to be a wife. Not ever again.

She still couldn't get over Jared's proposal. Her head was still reeling as she stood in front of the please be seated sign and glanced around for a friendly face.

The Starlight Diner was only half full on this Sunday morning, but it was early yet. They had the best brunch anywhere in all of Chestnut Grove. The funky ambiance added to the fun—the retro fifties motif and classic movie memorabilia lined the walls. The old-time jukebox crooned an Elvis classic.

"Meg, honey," said Sandra Lange, the owner of the snazzy little place, popped through the kitchen doors loaded down with a full tray. "Anne's all the way in the back."

"Thanks." Meg held a soft spot for the waitress who'd served her and her friends nearly every Sunday brunch for too many years to count. Recently, the woman had been diagnosed with breast cancer. She seemed to be holding her own, although that had to be a painful battle, and one that she seemed to be doing alone.

Alone. It was a blessing after a marriage like hers, Meg realized, but the other side of it was frightening. An accident or an illness, it was a lot to handle alone. And if she was hit by a bus or fell suddenly ill, who would take care of Luke? Her mom couldn't be counted on. Not really.

"Meg!" Anne popped up over the back of the tall vinyl booth, thankfully interrupting Meg's macabre thoughts.

Dear Anne. Her spirits lifted at the sight of her friend. She turned the corner, following the aisle, and the booth came into sight. Rachel, just arrived, was across the Formica tabletop from Anne, taking off her sunglasses and slipping them into their fine leather case. She looked elegant as always in a designer outfit that didn't come across as the least bit ostentatious in the modest diner.

"Oh, I have something for your little boy." Rachel dug in her handbag and pulled out a neatly folded toddler sized T-shirt. "They were selling these at the gala, and since I decided to get one for Gracie, I picked one up for Luke, too. It's for a good cause, so I couldn't resist."

Meg noticed the colorful decal on the plain white T-shirt, advertising Tiny Blessings with a child's choo-choo train beneath the lettering. "He'll love this. Thanks. I noticed your folks had her with them at the gala, but I didn't get a chance to say hi to them. Is she still doing well?"

"She's thriving and happy," Rachel said of her one-year-old sister her parents had adopted. "My parents are thrilled."

"They looked happy." Meg stowed her bag on the floor, aware of Anne's silence and her concerned gaze. Meg's chest tightened. *Please don't mention the boys' situation.* It was all she could do to hold it together. She wasn't ready to talk about it, because she realized that Jared was right. There was no easy solution to their problem. Except his solution, which was not simple at all.

With a hush of rubber-soled shoes, Sandra bustled over and slid two pots of steaming tea on the table, along with a carafe of coffee. "Are you girls doin' the buffet this morning?"

"You know we are," Meg answered.

"Then you girls help yourselves." The middle-aged lady was efficient as she slipped the extra creamer and sugar on the table beside the steaming beverage pots. "Give me a holler if you need any little thing."

"Thanks, Sandra," they all chimed.

Meg watched the woman in her trademark pink, ruffled diner apron with an embroidered *S* on her right shoulder turn, give them all a maternal nod and then go on her way.

Sadness seemed to follow her, and Meg recognized another woman who was battle-scarred at a deep level.

Since no ring marked Sandra's left hand, she wondered what heartache had wounded the woman's spirit. Probably a man, Meg reasoned as Anne and Rachel reached to fill their cups.

"Meg, tea?" Anne offered, sweet as always, and poured.

"Thanks."

"She always seems so sad," Anne commented as she filled Meg's cup.

"I was just thinking the same thing." Meg thanked her and reached for the sugar canister.

"Sort of like you." Gentle, those words, as Anne cradled the steaming cup in her hands.

"Everyone has their sorrows," Meg replied, with a quick glance at Rachel.

Rachel had lost her college sweetheart in a motorcycle accident and had moved away, for a time, from the area. Anne and Pilar had troubles and lives of their own, and were dedicated to their work at Tiny Blessings.

"Yes," Anne countered, "but some have more than others. Rachel, did you get a chance to see Jared Kierney's little boy?"

"No, I was pretty busy. I didn't know he had a son."

"Not just any son. A little boy he adopted from Tiny Blessings. One who is identical to Meg's Luke."

"What?"

Meg nodded, misery digging deep. "They're twins, according to the records Kelly found yesterday. They should have been placed together."

"That's why Pilar and I have started to help Kelly go through all the records. We haven't gone far and already we've found a lot of clerical mistakes, though nothing yet as serious as what happened in your situation. It raises a lot of questions."

Questions Meg feared could destroy what was the most important part of her world. Luke was her everything.

"At the very least," Rachel sympathized, "there's a little boy he should be growing up with."

"Exactly." Meg's chest hitched. "I'd like to say Luke is too little to understand that he has a brother, but it's not true."

"I've watched a lot of specials about twins," Anne commented, setting down her cup. "It's amazing. They have a bond that normal siblings don't even share. Or, at least, they can. Even twins separated at birth."

"Oh, that's the real dilemma." Remembering how the boys had seemed to instantly communicate made the pain inside her expand until she couldn't breathe.

The thought of admitting that Jared was right terrified her. And worse, she'd fallen away from God, or at least, she could no longer feel Him. But she had to try. *God, if You're out there, You have to know. Luke is all I have left. He's my everything.*

She heard nothing. She couldn't feel Him.

Maybe she would never feel Him again. But if He was there somewhere, then He had to know she felt as if she were lost at sea treading water with no sight of shore or a ship or any possible rescue. And it was all she could do to catch her next breath.

She wasn't complaining. But she was drowning, and the thought of embarking on another marriage renewed a panic within her she couldn't explain. She was still lost from the first shipwreck of a marriage. She didn't have enough strength or belief or faith in anyone to go through that again.

She covered her face, because she didn't want them to begin to see the bleak sea she was lost in. It was her own fault and there was nothing that could do about it.

Not even God could change the past, so why was He putting this in her life?

I'm trying to understand. I'm trying to hear You. She took a ragged breath. Maybe God wasn't really there at all. Or maybe she'd blown her chance with Him.

Suddenly Pilar was there, sliding into the booth alongside Anne. "Good morning, *amigas*. Church was awesome this morning. How are you all doing?"

"We're talking about Meg's adoption quandary," Rachel explained.

"This is all going to work out for the best, you'll see," Pilar encouraged.

"We'll stand beside you all the way," Anne added.

Meg felt her pain brim over, no matter how hard she held it back. Maybe it wasn't pain at all, it was simply gratitude, and that came with its own sweet aching. What would she do without her friends?

"It's going to be all right." Pilar hopped up and scooted next to her on the edge of the bench seat and squeezed her in a hug. "Don't be so sad, Meg."

How did she begin to explain? "I'm not sad, not with such wonderful women as my friends. Have I thanked you all lately?"

"Well, no better friends have probably existed, so that means we're all just lucky." Rachel slipped her arm around Meg's shoulders.

"We're the lucky ones," Anne agreed.

"Blessed," Pilar added.

At one time, Meg would have agreed, but her faith had faltered, or at least hit a mute button in concerns with the Lord, although understanding lingered in Pilar's gaze. Stalwart and honest, and Meg felt shamed.

Pilar had plenty of hardships in her life, but her faith was a solid foundation in her life. *Is it just me,* she wondered. *What do I need to do differently to hear You?*

Sandra returned, her gaze kindly as she slipped a steamy drink onto the edge of the table. "I don't mean to interrupt. Pilar, dear, here's your usual. You girls look sad. Is there something I can do to help?"

It was hard to miss the quiet sympathy the tired-looking woman was offering. Meg was touched. "I just learned my son has a brother. That sounds confusing, doesn't it? What I mean is, I adopted Luke when he was two days old."

"Oh, you adopted your little boy?" Sandra's eyes filled. "I remember you brought him in the other night for a chocolate milk shake. He sure was a sweetheart. What a blessing you must be to him."

"He's the blessing." Meg's entire soul warmed simply from thinking of him. Her precious son. She would do anything for him. Anything. Even open the wounds of the past and endure worse, if it would make him happy.

She was vaguely aware of Sandra saying she'd pray for them. Sandra patted Meg's hand and padded away, but she was lost in her thoughts. Consider marrying again? Her stomach twisted into knots. Not even her favorite cup of tea could soothe it away.

"I can't believe you're leaving right now. And you're not just going out of town, but you're leaving the country."

Jared bristled at the censure in his mom's voice,

probably because he knew she was right. Very right. It wasn't the best time to leave, but he dropped another pair of trousers, pleated and ironed, on the top of his suitcase and tossed the empty hangers onto the far end of his bed. "My job requires some travel. It's not like I have a lot of choice."

"You always have a choice."

"I won't be gone long." A few days in Geneva, it was the kind of assignment he'd been praying for. The timing was the problem. He'd asked to be reassigned, but he'd practically groveled for this assignment. He'd stuck close to home after the dark times grieving Vanessa.

He'd struggled to get by and to get Chance through his grief, too, and he thought the two of them were starting to hit an even keel. And now, he'd gotten hit with this twist. How could anyone have made an honest mistake by separating two identical twins? It felt like a blow to the solar plexus and Jared wanted to stay and sort it out, but there was only one good solution.

He remembered the look on Meg's face when he'd proposed. *Lord, I don't think she's going to change her mind.*

He sorted through his tie rack, ignoring the frown he knew was on his mother's face. He could practically hear her thoughts. She was right, but going out of town for less than a week wasn't going to make a difference in this situation, and it would cause a hardship for his boss. "I can't cancel at this late notice. I can't do that to Rick."

"Can't. It's a word. You can cancel if you want to."

"It's complicated." He dropped the ties on top of the slacks. He hated it when his mom was mad at him.

After her stroke, he'd been afraid she might never recover. That he'd lose her, too. He wanted to treasure this time with her, but that didn't mean they were always going to see eye to eye. Or change the fact that she still thought she could mother him as if he were a child.

"I gave my word. I'm not going to break it. I'm filling in last minute as it is."

"They found you last minute. They can find someone else. This is your son."

"Chance is fine. He's great. You'll be with him. And the baby sitter will be here during the day to help out. I'll be back home on Saturday."

"What are you going to do about Meg?"

"There's nothing to do about Meg." He hunted through the closet for his white shirts. He found blue, off-white, tan, brown and black. Where were the whites?

That's what he got for packing at the last second. "Have you seen my—oh, there they are."

Purposefully keeping his distance, he eased around his mother, who was giving him the hairy eyeball, as she always called it, when he'd been a particularly bad boy.

He was a man now. There was no earthly reason why her hairy eyeball should make him feel like going to sit in the corner and think about what he'd done. He'd done nothing wrong. "I'm going to do my job. People travel for their occupations all the time. Stop scolding me with that silent thing you do."

"What thing?"

"Now you're arching your brow."

"Well, the hairy eyeball wasn't working."

He rolled his eyes. His mother! "What do you want me to do? The boys are brothers. It's official. Whether I fly to Switzerland or not isn't going to change the outcome."

"But what are you going to do, just go on as if you didn't know anything about this?"

There was more to it, something much deeper that his mother wasn't admitting to, and he thought he knew what it was. "Chance is your only grandchild."

"Not truly. There is one more little boy and I...I saw them together. I took care of Luke briefly at the celebration. He's just as dear as Chance. In fact, he's just like Chance. How could I not love him?" She sighed, looking a little watery. "I just keep wishing this was a perfect world God created for us."

"God created this earth to be just what it is. It's not supposed to be perfect. Only God is that." He brushed a kiss on his mother's cheek, and affection lit him up. Yeah, he loved his mom.

He didn't want to see her sad. "I spoke to Meg this morning. And I don't know for sure, but I would guess she'll let you see Luke, if you'd like to ask her. She seems all alone, although her family is right here in town."

"It's sad, too. Meg's a fine young woman. And to think of what I heard from the fallout of their divorce! Not that I'm nosy or a gossip! But my heart broke when I heard. Eddie had all of us at church fooled, but her most of all."

"That's the way I figured it." Jared couldn't stomach even thinking of a man who would cheat on his wife, because the truth was, that was also cheating on a sacred vow to God and causing the woman he professed to love severe heartbreak.

All he needed to do was look at Meg, and he could

see it. This morning on her front porch, in her gentle presence, he'd *felt* it. Eddie had done more than betray her. He'd wounded the very foundation of who she was. Her confidence, her heart, her soul *and* her belief.

No wonder she turned him down flat. His chest constricted and he felt lost. He felt as if he didn't know which way to turn and was trusting in the Lord to point him in the right direction.

God is ever gracious, and Jared had been able to find firm footing and rebuild his life. For his son's sake. And for Vanessa, who had to be watching over them from above.

This had to work out, it had to. But how? Raising the brothers in two separate households? That was no solution. Marriage? It would at least satisfy the original conditions of the adoption, but Meg was so set against it, even for the boys' sake.

I know we can make it work. He felt it to the very inner part of his soul.

Back in high school, he'd had a huge crush on Meg. But now, he couldn't deny the beginning flutters of love. And it was surprising that after all he'd been through, he could feel romantic love again.

What about Meg? Was there a chance that she could love again? If not, then what about their boys?

"I hear it wasn't just the one affair that Eddie Talbot had." Mom's words came strained, and not only snagged him out of his thoughts, but stunned him, too.

Eddie had cheated on Meg *more* than once? Did that mean she'd taken him back and forgiven him, only to be betrayed again? No wonder she was so adamantly against marriage. No wonder she was so hurt.

He sank on the edge of the bed, abandoning his hunt

for enough pairs of clean dark socks. He sat there, his thoughts beginning to spin away. It all made sense. He'd imagined that one affair was enough to break any-one to the core, but numerous times? How deeply did that hurt a woman?

There simply was no chance that she would change her mind. Absolutely none.

"I'm glad you told me about that." Feeling grim, he rubbed his face with his hand.

He was tired, he was wrung out, but mostly he was sickened. Meg only came alive for her son, and even then, he could see the strain. That she was more a shell of a woman than whole and alive.

Sadness ebbed into his spirit, weighing him down, on this evening when he ought to be excited. He was fi-nally getting a choice assignment. And yet, it didn't seem as great as it had when his supervisor had ap-proached him about it last week.

Leaving his son was always hard enough, but he couldn't get away from the feeling he'd lost something of immense value. Not only the chance to be married to Meg. But something grander. Something of vital impor-tance.

He realized it was his first love he'd lost. That he'd always tucked the sweetness of his first crush away in the corner of his heart. For safekeeping. He'd gone on, found deep love and married another. And if Vanessa had lived, then he never would have taken out that mem-ory and wondered.

But he had. And now it was gone forever. Broken by a man he didn't even know. By Eddie Talbot, who'd taught Meg that marriage was about lies and deceit, hurt and betrayal. And what could ever make her want to try again? Especially so soon after a devastating, wrenching divorce? Nothing.

Defeated, he got to his feet and went in search of his socks, knowing that it was going to be a long night. Another one without a lot of sleep and even less hope.

Chapter Six

Exhausted from a long, trying day at work, Meg staggered through the front door while Luke was whimpering with his arms so tight around her neck, she thought he was going to take off her skin. Poor baby. She kissed his forehead as she put him down in the foyer where two of the cats were protesting the late hour.

"I know. I'll get to you two in a second." She slid her briefcase on the hall table and wasn't at all surprised when the cats stalked off, tails swishing, at the rain pelting off her jacket.

Yeah, it had been that kind of a day. Enough had gone wrong—meetings gone late, budgetary disasters and a major client threatened to jump to another agency. Add to that the remnants of a tropical storm that had kicked up just before four-thirty and the commute had been a nightmare. At least she was home. The worst was over. She knelt to free Luke from his little rain slicker and the lights flickered once, twice, then stayed out.

Okay, she had been wrong—now it was worse.

Luke gave an enthusiastic "Uh-oh!" and clapped his

hands. It was a rather wet sound. His shoes swished and squeaked on the tile entry—he'd had to stomp in every puddle they'd come across until she'd picked him up, shrieking in protest, to avoid more splashing.

She hadn't been able to keep him calm during the quick dash down the crowded aisles of the grocery store. He'd had a meltdown in front of the bakery section and almost another one in the checkout line. Her debit card had refused to work for no apparent reason.

It was hard doing everything alone, but this day was still better than any one of the days when she was married. Meg shrugged out of her dripping coat and felt for the flashlight that was supposed to be handy on the top shelf of the entry closet. Supposed to be, being the key word. Her fingertips found nothing but air and last winter's wool gloves.

Luke had dashed off, his feet pounding and squishing on the hardwood floor and echoing in the living room. She followed him into the room, located the match tin on the upper shelf of the entertainment center and lit the candles set out on a wrought-iron holder that held five citrus-scented candles. The flame tossed a warm reflection in the mirror above the mantle.

Luke's footsteps halted beside her. "Ooh! Oo-ooh!"

"No fire for you, baby boy." Leaving the candles safely flickering, she headed for the kitchen. "Is your tummy hungry?"

"Yep! Cookie!"

Rain pummeled like hail and she thought about the ingredients for a tuna casserole in the back of her minivan in the detached garage. The one good thing about this weather was she didn't have to go back out in the storm for the groceries since there was no way to use the oven. She reached for the phone instead.

But wait, with no power that meant the little delivery place down the street and around the corner was probably in the dark, too. Her stomach growled and before she could consider what other dinner options she had, her cell rang. "Hello?"

"Meg, this is Donna, Jared's mom. Is this a bad time?"

"Mrs. Kierney, it's never a bad time to hear from you." Meg had always adored the woman, who was warm and caring and always had a kind word. She peeked in on Luke, who was still chasing his shadow around the living room. "What can I do for you?"

"Goodness, I wanted to ask about helping *you*. Jared said it would be all right if I called and oh, now, I hope you haven't had a chance to make dinner. That was part of my plan."

"Your plan? What plan would that be?"

"The one where I bring a nice delicious meal as a guise to see, well, I guess it would be my honorary grandchild. I hope you don't mind, but my heart is just taken with your little one, too. Tell me if this worries you at all. If you'd rather I kept my distance, I'll respect that, but getting time to come to know your Luke would just do this old sick woman a world of good."

"You looked vibrant and healthy the last time I saw you."

"Well, life is uncertain, dear. You never know."

Meg couldn't hold that well-intended manipulation against her. There was not a nicer lady alive. Donna's kindness was not a problem. "Come on over, and you don't need to bring food."

"Oh, I intended to make myself welcome, and I remember what it was like to be a working mother. I worked when Jared was a boy, too. You don't mind if I bring Chance with me, do you? Just say the word and I'll leave him with the sitter, but it would sure be nice to see them together."

"You are a master plotter."

"Don't I know it, sugar. I'll be over in a few minutes."

"It's raining too hard to go out."

"I'm fearless. Don't you worry."

Meg hung up the phone. What an unexpected bonus. She hoisted Mercy onto the top ledge of her carpeted kitty condo and swept into the kitchen, matchbox in hand, to light the decorative votives she kept around the eating nook. The light was enough to dig through the junk drawer and find a small flashlight.

"Wee!" Luke called out. "Mama! Weeee!"

She looked up to see Luke spinning in circles with his blanky over his head.

"Hey, little man. Are you getting dizzy?" She knelt to pluck the blanket off his head and he rewarded her with a wide, dazzling grin.

Oh, I love you, little boy. Her entire being shone bright like the first light of a new day, so lovely it was hard to see the shadows. "Mrs. Kierney's coming. And Chance. Do you remember Chance?"

"Bop!" Luke offered another grin and stole his blanky back from her. He draped it over his head and took off, barreling down the short hallway, making the dishes in the hutch rattle.

The doorbell rang above the crash of thunder overhead, which shook the dishes some more.

"Whozzit?" Luke changed direction and raced to the door.

She had to run to reach the door first, not that he

could open the doorknob—yet. She took him by the shoulder, backing him against her shins so she could open up. Rain punched and gushed from the porch roof, and overflowed from the gutters, but in the bold light of a handheld lantern, Mrs. Kierney leaned on her cane in the shelter of the porch roof. She had Luke's twin by the hand. Behind her was a young woman, who held both a diaper bag and an insulated hamper.

"Uh!" Chance greeted.

"Hello, little guy, Donna. Come in, quick!" Meg reached for the lantern, shuffling her flashlight to the entry table. "I can't believe you wanted to come out in this."

"I'm a stubborn woman. I made up my mind to come, if you would allow me to, and no storm short of an all-out hurricane can stop me." Donna softened her words with a gentle smile, stepping inside and aside so that her grandchild and the babysitter were all dry. "Why, hello there, Luke. I'm your Gramma Donna. What do you think about that?"

"Bop!" Luke offered his most charming smile beneath the fraying hem of his train motif baby blanket.

"Chance, you come play with your brother. And Leeza, just put that down. You go on home now."

"Sure thing, Mrs. Kierney." The young woman, who Meg vaguely recognized as someone from the Community Church, set the hamper and bag down, said a pleasant good-night and rushed out into the storm, obviously eager to make it home before it became any worse.

Meg battled the winds to shut the door and heard Luke's voice say, "Ey?"

When she turned to look, it wasn't Luke, it was Chance. It was strange—good strange—but different to see two of them. She watched spellbound, unable to look away from this little person so like her little boy. Chance dropped to his knees and drove his hand into the open top of the diaper bag. He fished around while Luke watched entranced. Then with a sound of victory, he hauled out a tattered baby blanket. He grinned wide and happily dropped the blanket over his head.

"Bop!" Luke shouted.

"Ey!" Chance answered.

They both lifted up the hems of their blankets and laughed when they saw each other.

"Notice the blankets." Donna sidled close.

In the golden haze of the lantern light, Meg saw it clearly. The printed bright trains, trestles and depots that was the same exact pattern as the one Luke had. The same exact blanket.

"The Lord works in mysterious ways." Donna seemed to find her statement self-explanatory as she went to lift the hamper.

Meg caught her by the shoulder. "This is my job, because you're my guest. Why don't you go watch the boys play in the living room? Put your feet up and just enjoy the twins."

"That would be lovely, dear. Oh, to see them together. To think. Both of them are going to be mine. Come, boys. Luke, come show Gramma Donna your toys."

"Bop!" Luke covered his head and took one giant hop.

"Bop!" Chance mimicked.

Too cute. By all accounts, Meg shouldn't be so charmed by this. The boys did belong together, and a loving grandmother was a true gift to Luke. He preened at the attention, and it was heartening to see, when he'd been sad for so long missing Eddie.

Family. That's what every child needed, Meg knew. Donna's loving voice and Luke's happy laughter followed her into the kitchen, where she unloaded the hamper. The delicious scents of fried chicken and coleslaw, buttery mashed potatoes and baked beans, made the kitchen seem cozy. When had her mom brought supper over, wanting to spend time with Luke? Never. When had Sue Ellen made Luke giggle so joyfully? Never.

Maybe Jared had a point. "I can offer your son something he's never had. A real man for a father. A man who will love him and treasure him." Jared's words swirled like smoke from the flickering candles, hazy and ethereal and dissipating into nothing, nothing at all.

How do I know if I can trust you, Jared? The pit of her stomach burned. She'd vowed never to trust any man again. And, she admitted, with the way she kept everyone at an arm's length, maybe she would never really trust anyone again.

She felt as if she were holding on to a two-thousand-piece puzzle and all the pieces were slipping through her fingers. She knew for absolute certain that several vital pieces were missing, forever gone. And no matter what she did or how hard she tried, she could never make whole the pieces of her life.

"Meg? Do you want me to get that, sweetie?" Donna called from the other room, above the happy screeches of two active little boys. "Your phone is ringing."

"Oh, I'll grab it. You just enjoy the boys." Sure enough, she could hear the musical jangle of her cell phone, although it was hard to hear with the storm battering the house and the noise of two boys racing around the living room. "Hello?"

Static answered, and then Jared's deep baritone. "Meg? Can you hear me?"

"Why are you calling? I mean—" Realizing how that had to have sounded, she cleared the emotion from her throat. "I'm just surprised. Oh, are you looking for your mom?"

"No, I wanted to talk to you. Why? Did she keep her threat to come visit you?"

"She's here right now, saving the day for me. She's watching the boys while I set the table." Speaking of which, she hurried back to the kitchen and counted out flatware from the top drawer. "Are you having second thoughts about your proposition?"

"It was no proposition. It was a proposal. And yes, I am having second thoughts."

She half expected this, she admitted as she laid flatware and plates on the round oak table in the shadowed nook. "It's all right. I understand. We both know what marriage really is. It's a lot different from what they tell you when you're young and naive enough to believe it."

An ocean and a continent away, Jared winced at her words that were not bitter, but spoken as if she were wise, as if she'd experienced a truth about life that everyone came to know in time. He thought of the contentedness he knew with Vanessa, of the happy moments and the tenderness, and the harder times, too. Life was no picnic sometimes, but no matter how hard things got, they had gotten through them, together, side by side. *That* was the sort of marriage God had in mind for His faithful. Not the kind of union that brought pain and endless sadness.

He felt sick. For her. For their boys. He tried to think of the best way to say what was on his mind. "I suppose any marriage depends on what the man and woman bring to their relationship. And I guess that's why I called. I'm having second thoughts about giving you an ultimatum, not over the proposal."

"What? But I thought you'd changed your mind."

"No, I still want to marry you. I told you I'd accept your decision on Saturday, when I get back, yes or no. But I was wrong. Marriage is a serious commitment, and I shouldn't have pressured you. I don't ever want to hurt you."

"Then what are you trying to do?"

She sounded confused, and he couldn't imagine what she expected. Did she think that he would try to hurt her on purpose? That wasn't what he had in mind at all. Was that her expectation of him? Or was it what she'd learned as Eddie Talbot's wife?

His chest ached as if a double-edged blade had dug deep between the chambers of his heart. "I should have said something to you before I left. It's been troubling me, and I regret the way I must have sounded. It wasn't what I meant."

He sounded so honest, Meg thought. She swallowed hard, surprised by the unexpected sob in her throat. "Say that again."

"I'm sorry." He sounded sincere.

She believed him. "I meant the part about hurting me."

"I never want to hurt you. Ever. I will promise you this. Whether you marry me or not, I will never intentionally hurt you in any way. And if I'm a big dope and do it by mistake, then you have the right to call me on it and make me grovel, until I've made everything all right."

"How do you feel about ashes and sackcloth?"

He chuckled. "I'm okay with that."

Lightning strobed through the house, flashing her shadow on the floor at her feet. Realizing she'd been standing idle, she began to move around the table, setting four places. Considering his words, she went to drag the bar chair from the center island for a second high chair, and stopped midway when Jared spoke.

"I said how I could be a real father to your Luke. I'd love him the same, I swear. I'd be strong and kind and steady. You know that about me, don't you?"

"I can see you're an excellent father to Chance."

"I try my best. I'm someone you can count on. I won't be like your son's father and just walk away. I'll be a father that stays and stands tall, for his sake. I travel for my job sometimes, but I'll be there to coach baseball and I won't miss a football game. You know all this, right?"

"I know you're a decent person, Jared. That isn't what's at issue." How did she say she was going down for the third time, feeling the water rush over her head and the fathomless ocean pulling her down? That's what marriage had been for her.

Then he paused to clear his throat. "What I didn't say is that Chance lost his mother. He was too young, a lot of people said, to really know that he'd lost her. But he knew. She was his mom, his caretaker, and he was her entire world. It's been a tough haul for him without her. He has my love, but it's only half of what he deserves."

I know what you're going to say next, Jared Kierney. She tried to close off her ears so she wouldn't hear and her emotions so she wouldn't feel, but the power of his words bowled her over just the same.

"I don't think Chance could have a better mom than you. That's all I have to say. Just please, carefully consider it. For their sakes."

Like a punch to her chest, the air whooshed out of her lungs and she let go of the chair to cover her mouth. But she couldn't keep the agony inside.

Maybe it was the ghost of Eddie's words criticizing her, always criticizing, how she was a poor mother, she was too soft, she was spoiling the boy, she wasn't teaching him discipline. And to hear Jared's approval hit her right where it mattered. Her emotions rose to the surface and the cynic in her wanted to say that Jared was just saying whatever it took to get her to do what he wanted.

But, no, that wasn't right. She wished she could doubt his honesty, but it rang so clear and true it was impossible to deny. She'd never much thought about adopting another child, especially after her divorce. It seemed to take everything out of her, but she loved being a mother. And to think of Chance needing her made longing rip painfully through her. The line filled with more static as she fought to catch her composure.

"Meg, are you all right? Please. You can talk to me."

His concern only made the torture within her sharpen. She felt as if she'd been going down for the third time and suddenly the ocean had released its grip on her. Air rushed into her lungs and gratitude surged into her lonely heart.

"Meg? Meg?"

"I'm okay," she managed to choke out the same moment two pairs of little feet pounded into the kitchen. At her weakest moment, in they came. The reason for all this turmoil. Luke was holding his blanket in one hand and his plastic train engine in the other. A few inches behind him came his double image holding the matching plastic caboose.

Laughing together, the two little boys skidded to a stop in front of her. Looked up at her with glee, and then turned tail and scurried off, running straight to their grandmother in the living room. Luke first, with Chance a step behind, identical cowlicks, exact same patter of feet, brothers, by blood and by birth and by right.

For their sake, she took another gulp of air and said the words that made her cold inside. "I've made up my mind."

"Are you sure? I mean, I don't want you to be hasty. I know how you feel about marrying again, but I keep hoping if you think about it long enough, you'll begin to see that this isn't such a bad idea. I'd treat you right, Meg—"

As well as any man probably could, she thought. And that wasn't better than being alone. No. She took a look around her kitchen. Arranged, just the way she wanted it. Nothing was wrong by any one else's standards. Being single was terribly nice. A relief from a life of trying to compromise and do what was best for her husband, and always being the one to give. And give in. And give up. She'd tried her hardest but she could never make Eddie happy. Eventually, there just wasn't enough of her left.

I just can't do it again. I can't, God.

There was no answer in the storm and the night, except for two little boys, one chasing the other, alike in every way.

She may not be able to hear God, Meg realized, but she had eyes to see. She loved her son more than her happiness. And Chance, who skidded to a stop in front of her, gazed with big soulful eyes so like Luke's, but he was different, too. A little boy with no mother just begging to be loved.

Her heart wrenched, and she said the words that would seal her unhappiness forever. But think of what it would do for the twins, she told herself. "I've decided to accept your offer."

"You're *what?* You…you're going to marry me?"

She sighed, feeling the water begin to tug her back down. She had to fight for air and fight to breathe. He sounded so incredulous and happy. Maybe, for men, marriage was easier. "I'll meet your flight on Saturday. Your mom has all the info?"

"Yeah. Wow. Meg, we can make this good for both of us. I'm glad you can see that. We already have two great reasons pulling for us. Our sons."

"We do." Her hand was shaking so badly, she had trouble holding the phone. The connection was getting worse, due to the international call or the storm, it didn't matter which. She was glad to have an excuse to tell him goodbye and end the call.

Chance and Luke made a final revolution before skidding to a halt in the shadowy nook. The boys looked at each other and stared for a moment, as if they were communicating. Innocent sweetness and pure joy filled the room.

Chance pointed at the ceiling. "Uh?"

"Ha!" Luke answered and they giggled together as if they'd shared a great joke.

Our sons, Jared had said.

"Is everything all right, dear?"

Meg looked up, surprised to see that Donna had ambled into the nook, radiating concern. Real concern.

"I think I'm going to be better, thanks."

Donna only confirmed her decision. Luke needed a grandmother like her. He ran to her, already trusting her, and gave her a charming look that had her more adoring, if she wasn't enough all ready. A child can never have too much love or family members who thought they were the most special child ever.

This is already better for him, she thought as she finished setting the table. And out of the corner of her eye, she watched as Donna held out her free hand to the little ones. "Come, boys, let's get you washed up for supper."

"No! No! No!" Luke shouted his favorite word with joy.

"Yes! Yes! Yes!" Donna looked up with a question, to which Meg answered by pointing down the hall. The doting grandmother steered the toddlers toward the main floor bathroom, leaving Meg alone. But not lonely. Not without hope. This is a definite improvement, she thought. As long as she didn't think about marrying again, she was able to see the bright side.

It was the other side, the hidden darker side, of marriage—and of trusting a man—that she didn't want to think about. She was certain Jared would be all that Luke could need in a father.

No, Jared loved being a father. Some men were born to be dads and Jared was one of them. She could count on him with her son's heart.

But she would never trust him with her own.

Chapter Seven

Lord, don't let her change her mind.

Jared had nothing else in his thoughts during the long journey home. Airport lines and security and layovers meant plenty of downtime with which to think. Then there were more lines and security and layovers. By the time his flight touched down on the runaway at Richmond airport, he was too exhausted to think straight, but one thought sustained him.

He'd be hearing her voice as soon as the pilot gave the word it was safe to use cell phones. He felt like he'd waited long enough, thank you, but he complied. When the plane decelerated, lightly pressing him back into his businessclass seat, he felt a zip of something that felt like gladness at the thought of hearing Meg's voice.

He was dialing the nanosecond the pilot gave the okay, and she answered on the second ring. He could hear the rush of traffic. "You must be on the freeway."

"Taking the airport exit right now. I know I'm running a few minutes late, but I was stuck in a meeting."

"On Saturday morning? I get that a lot, too. Well,

Meg, I think we have a lot in common. Do you think we can juggle two careers with our family?"

She paused, and he wondered what he'd said that had quieted her. But she said in that soft way of hers, "I was hoping we could. I love my job, and it's more than that. I don't want to rely on you. I know that sounds bad—"

Jared felt her pain, a pain that seemed to be fathomless. "No. I understand. You have a job that matters to you, and between the two of us, we can work this all out. We're intelligent and reasonable people, and I just want you to be happy."

"We are going to have a lot to work out, I'm afraid. Which house do we keep? What about day care? That's just the start."

"I know. We can talk about this kind of thing on the way home, so I don't want you to worry, okay?"

She paused, and he felt her relief radiate across the miles. They made arrangements to meet outside baggage claim, and he tucked his phone away.

Wow, he was marrying Meg Kramer. Talbot now, but not for long. Meg Kierney. Mom would be ecstatic, but he resisted the urge to call. He was dying to talk to Chance and of sharing his news, but he would take care of Meg first. She was afraid. He'd recognized the thin emotional quality in her voice, and he didn't blame her. If what Mom had said about her marriage was true, and it probably was, then her marriage had been a sad one. He didn't blame her for balking at the idea of a sudden, convenient marriage.

While they were not perfect strangers, a lot of time had passed and they'd both loved and lost, for different reasons and with different outcomes. But to the core of his being, he believed marrying Meg was the right decision. The boys would grow up as brothers, as the Lord meant them to be.

This can work. This has to. Chance and Luke deserved a loving family. And Jared would do his best to make sure of it.

As the plane bumped to a stop and passengers hopped to their feet, grabbing stowed luggage although there was nowhere to go, he remained seated. He kept thinking of the boys and of Meg the entire time. Finally the line began to move forward and he stood.

It felt as if unknown forces were keeping him back as he wound his way through the airport to baggage claim. And then he endured the inordinate wait until the flight's baggage came churning down. His suitcases were some of the last to be released. He fought back the frustration, because the truth was, he hadn't realized how much he wanted to see Meg again.

But each moment stretched like a rubber band tighter and tighter in his chest until it was a physical pain. The instant he stepped outside into the glaring humidity, a horn caught his attention and there she was. An unexpected punch of joy rippled through him. Surprised, he didn't know what to make of it as he watched her minivan pull to the curb. The side door slid open.

Amazement slid over him. Here she was, picking him up—his fiancée. Wow. Meg. The woman who'd captivated him completely so long ago was going to be his wife. He was going to have to get over the glory of it sometime, but not yet and not today. Happiness filled him up, spilling over, and it was nothing short of a blessing. Did she feel God's hand in this, too?

He loaded his bags, hardly aware of what he was doing. All he could see was her dear face watching him over the bucket seat, her soft red hair burnished by the sun and her jeweled blue eyes tight with worry.

She looked unhappy. How much had she worked herself up over agreeing to marry him? His guts clenched tight and he saw the evidence on her face. The dark circles. The lines creased around her soft rosebud mouth. The sadness in her heart that he could feel, like a winter's freezing mist eking into his soul.

If only she were pleased about their engagement.

Lord, I'm asking you to guide me. Please show me the right way to handle this. Trusting the Father to lend him a hand, Jared hopped in the passenger seat and buckled up. He swore he could feel the sunshine strengthen and along with it, the certainty of the Lord's answer.

It was simple. First Corinthians. "Love is patient. Love is kind." Those were the first steps he needed to take. And in all honesty, that was what was in his heart. He saw the tension tight in Meg's jaw and in her hands as she gripped the gearshift too tightly and slid it into drive.

"All set?" She looked as if she were bracing herself for a trip into a war zone instead of a pleasant drive to his townhouse on the outskirts of Richmond.

There was no reason for her to be anxious. None at all. "I am. I sure appreciate your coming to fetch me."

"It will give us time to talk. Unfortunately—" She paused while she checked her side mirror and pulled back into the moving line of traffic. "There was a crisis at work this past week and I have to get back to the office. I had hoped we would have time to really talk before we had to face this. I know you're probably beat."

"You should have told me if picking me up was inconvenient—"

"Oh, it's not. I just can't stay and talk about our... well, our wedding." She nearly choked on the word. "This isn't how I was envisioning today. I'm sorry."

"Don't apologize. I understand. I have an idea. If you trust me, that is. Do you?"

She glanced at him sideways before turning her attention back to the road. "I'm not sure. Should I trust you?"

"Absolutely. Why don't I drop you off at your office, so you can return to your meeting? Then give me a call and I'll come get you. I'll have Mom keep the boys a little later. You and I can have dinner. We can keep it casual, something easy so the both of us can wind down and we'll figure out what we're going to do."

Yeah, you seem harmless right now, buster. Meg knew she shouldn't be charmed into thinking they were on the same side. Marriage was like war. Two sides, and a battle ending with a winner. And a loser.

She tried to ignore the burning in her stomach. She was going to have to buy stronger antacids if she went through with this. No, she corrected herself, picturing Luke's adoring face as he'd basked in Jared's fatherly attention last week.

She *would* go through with this. "You want me to trust you with my brand-new minivan?"

"Sure. Since I'll be obligated to drive it on family outings, I may as well get used to handling it now." He grinned, and she realized she wasn't as immune to his dimpled smile as she wanted to be.

She didn't answer, and he kept right on talking. "Seriously, it's your call. I just figured if you have a crisis at work, then you need to get back ASAP instead of hauling my sorry self home. I don't mind coming to get you. In fact, I probably should drop by the office, and it's convenient on the way."

"You're being too helpful. I ought to be suspicious of you."

"Yep, you should. I just might be helpful again in the future. You never know."

"Husbands aren't helpful."

"Some husbands maybe. But some of us are stellar when it comes to husbandly duties."

Meg's eyes went wide.

Husbandly duties. Jared recognized his mistake in word choice too late. "I meant, like driving. Taking out the garbage. Mowing the lawn."

"Changing diapers?"

"I have extensive practice on that front."

Her white-knuckled grip on the steering wheel had eased, and he figured he was making progress. The first step was getting her to understand he wasn't going to hurt her.

The second was to convince her they were in this together. "Let's say we can grab some take-out on the way home. I don't know if you like Thai, but there's a great place just off Main."

"The one on the corner? They have the best noodles."

"I'll get an order of noodles and what else?"

"And cashew chicken?"

"You got it. I guess this counts as our first date."

"Our first and only." Meg signaled to merge onto the freeway, accelerating and watching traffic.

It gave her time to pretend to be concentrating on the heavy traffic when the truth was, she was surprised that their first meal together would be so compatible. Eddie had seemed to dislike everything she loved—then again, maybe he did that on purpose.

Please, let this be a sign that I'm not making a huge mistake. "We haven't talked about how soon you want to do this."

"When? Well, I thought we might want to have dinner, you know, around dinnertime."

She was not immune to the effect of his dimples, either. That wasn't good news. She couldn't imagine how on earth this was going to work. Although one thing she did appreciate was Jared's sense of humor. "I meant getting…married."

"'Married' isn't a dirty word."

"It is in my book."

"Then, baby, you were married to the wrong man. Wait until you're married to me."

"That's just what I like. A man who is humble." She merged into the middle lane to make better time to the downtown exits, enjoying the deep rumble of his chuckle.

"That's me. Modest to a fault. And very patient. In regards to your question, I want to get married right away. We can hop a commuter flight and get married tonight."

"You're kidding, right? Patient. That's a good one," she chuckled softly.

At least I've got you laughing, Jared thought, taking it as a sign that he was heading in the right direction. "Why wait? We've decided it's for the best. It might be good for the boys just to suddenly have us all together. Instead of being together and then in separate houses at night. It might be easier on us, too, since we both have pretty demanding jobs."

"I guess it's sensible. There is no real reason to wait." Her voice sounded small.

He sensed the tiny ember of hope inside her. Maybe she was wishing that this time it would be different.

It will be, he vowed. *As the Lord is my witness.* Nothing would ever make him break a promise to God. But did Meg know that? He would have to show her day by day until she believed. He resisted the urge to lay his hand on hers. He sensed she might not be ready for a bigger connection between them. Yet.

She eased the minivan to the unloading zone in front of her building and eased the transmission into Park. She'd wait and see, but Jared meant well, she knew that. He was a man, which meant he just didn't realize, perhaps, how it was from a woman's perspective.

"I'm reluctant to marry you, you know that, but it will make the boys happy." It was the only truthful thing she could say. "That would be worth anything."

"Exactly. We're on the same side on this. What do you say about this week sometime?" He opened his door.

"I'll look at my calendar and see when I have free time."

"Great. And give me a jingle when you want to come home. I'll phone in the food order. Deal?"

Oh, he looked harmless and manly and irresistible, perfect for a magazine model for an ad promoting family, commitment and promises kept. Everything a woman could want and believe in.

She'd stopped believing long ago. All she could do was her best. She left the engine running and grabbed her purse. "I'll call you."

"I'll answer."

Meg fought a suffocating sense of doom as she hopped out into the humid sunshine, but at least Jared could make her smile.

Later that day, bone-tired, Meg told herself there had to be some good things about marrying Jared. He was polite. Look how he held the screen door for her with his foot, so he could keep the plastic sacks containing the carryout cartons level.

He paid for the meal. He'd picked her up on time, just like he'd said. And their talk on the way home had been illuminating. Jared had been very flexible, like an equal. A helpmate. Although that might be too good to prove true.

"I am grateful to you for agreeing to move into my home." Meg fished through her key ring. "I'm just now starting to feel settled here."

"I'd hate to uproot both you and Luke so soon after your divorce and buying this place."

That's the part of Jared she feared was too good to be true—he was so understanding and fair. Then again, he'd always been a play-by-the-book kind of person, even in high school. Where Eddie had been a jock and, well, one of those popular boys.

She found her deadbolt key and unlocked the front door. "Then welcome home. It's a little small, but it's cozy."

"It's roomy for a bungalow and I love craftsman-style homes. And cats," he added.

Mercy was drowsing on the vent just inside and Meg had to be careful not to thump her by opening the door all the way.

"She's a good doorstop," Jared dared to tease.

Mercy studied him disdainfully before flicking her tail.

"You're in trouble now." Meg stole one of the food sacks from Jared. "Watch out. Cats have great memories and hold serious grudges."

"Great. Just don't let her know about my dog."

There he went, making her smile again when so many issues weighed heavily on her. She'd hardly gotten much sleep this week with all the worry. But Jared seemed fine with her keeping her job, and that had been a huge issue before with Eddie, she thought silently as she led the way to the kitchen, flicking on lights as she went. Shirley and Goodness were snoozing on the cushions on the bay window seat, where the cool air slid upward from the vent.

Neither feline moved, just opened their eyes a slit to study the newcomer. Since it was too hot, they did nothing more than flick their tails and go right back to snoozing.

"I don't seem to be real popular with your cats." Jared followed her around the corner of the island and set the food sack down on the counter. "They liked me before."

"That was before you mentioned having a dog."

Was that a twinkle of humor bright in her eyes? It was hard to tell, as she turned away to reach two dinner plates from the custom oak cabinets.

She didn't seem too upset about the addition of a dog. "You like dogs?"

"Who doesn't? What's he like?"

"Big and dopey."

The plates clinked against the granite countertop a little too hard. "How big of a dog? How dopey?"

One look around her tidy, everything-in-its-place kitchen was all it took for Jared to start laughing. "He's huge. He's clumsy. He's basically a walking disaster. No, make that a full-bore running disaster."

"Well, you know what they say. Like master, like dog."

A tiny quirk played in the corners of her mouth, otherwise he never would have guessed she was playing with him. "I could take offense to that, but Buster is a stellar guy. Loyal, friendly, always stand by you in a pinch."

She grabbed flatware. "I bet he's humble, too."

"How did you know?"

They laughed together as she laid out the forks and spoons and reached for the fridge. "Do you want soda or juice?"

"Juice would be great." He was already helping himself to her cupboard and when he didn't find what he was looking for moved on to the next set of doors.

Cold tingled down the back of her neck. She remembered the vow she'd made when she'd moved out of the house that was in Eddie's name. Never again would she let another man into her life. So what was she doing? There was a man helping himself to her good glasses, as if he belonged here. She fought the panicked urge to run. Her spirit felt as heavy as one of those huge barbells at the gym.

He began opening the containers instead of sitting down at the table and waiting to be served.

Meg was suspicious of that. Eddie had been so calm and helpful at first, too. As she fetched the juice and serving spoons, she watched Jared out of the corner of her eye. He'd set the container in the middle of the table and did something Eddie never did.

He held her chair for her, as gallant as any well-mannered gentleman from another era.

She couldn't help it. Her heart fluttered. She had to be careful not to forget. She knew for a fact that fairy tales did not exist. *Don't be foolish, Meg. Don't start believing in the impractical.*

His big masculine hands were gripping the white backs of the Windsor chair. Why had she never noticed before how solid and dependable his hands looked? As if he could fix any problem, or soothe away any worry.

She gulped down the sob of hope in her throat, ashamed that somehow somewhere inside her she longed for real love. For real passion. For a man strong enough to stand tall against the world and tender enough to be loving.

"You look surprised, Meg. Don't be. You forget, I come trained. Vanessa always took pride in breaking me in from a cocky college student to a capable husband."

"You break in a shoe."

"Training me, then. I suppose there'll be a few more things I'll have to get used to with you." He winked. "So, what about the church? We could have Reverend Fraser marry us."

"No, he married Eddie and I. I'm not sure I could…" *forget,* she wanted to say, but it wasn't the only truth. "It would not be a good association. I don't want to start something as risky as marriage in the same way."

"This isn't a risk. We have every reason to fight for a good life together. Our sons." He appeared so terribly gallant, just the way he stood as he held the chair for her, his words lingering in the silence between them.

Our sons. Maybe a marriage could work out all right between two parents who were devoted to their children. She eased into the chair he held, every fiber of her being aware of his closeness. The intimate feel of his presence seemed to wrap around her like a warm blanket.

He moved away, his clothes rustling and his shoes padding on the hardwood floor, he seemed to stir something long dormant within her soul.

"I don't want a big wedding and all that goes with it." She watched his reaction as he circled around to the other side of the table. He didn't appear to dislike her suggestion, so that was encouraging. "This is a second wedding for both of us. Let's just do something practical. We could go to City Hall and be married by a justice of the peace."

"That's certainly practical."

"This is a practical marriage, Jared."

"Then it's settled. We'll go to see the judge next week. Chance and I move in here." He folded his big frame into the chair and grinned at her across the table. "Are you sure you don't mind about our dog? He's an inside dog, since I've sort of spoiled him. A lot."

"It's not the dog I'm worried about."

"Hey! I'm house-trained, don't you worry. So, we've got the wedding figured out. Now, what about the move? I don't suppose there is a quiet corner somewhere I can use as a home office?"

"You work a lot of weekends?"

"When I have to, but I can do a lot of my work from home. With the two of us so busy, I'm hoping I can come home early a few days a week so I can spend some time with the boys. My work is pretty mobile. I've got a laptop I carry around."

"I think we can find a dark, damp corner to stow you in," she said with a small smile.

"Sweet. Do you mind if I say grace?" He knew that she'd dropped out of the church. Her Bible and devotional lay unread and gathering dust on her nightstand.

And still he wanted to say grace? She unfolded the decorated paper napkin and laid it neatly on her lap. "Uh…no, go ahead."

Jared bowed his head, his dark hair tumbling forward so she could see the top of his head. And the cowlick in the back where a shock stood straight up, tousled by the wind. It was oddly vulnerable, to see him like this, openhearted. His fingers clasped together, and he cleared his throat.

Her stomach fisted, but it was not Eddie's memory that came with the prayer. Jared's virtuous baritone held her here, in the present, reminding her of all the good things in her life. Her safe, comfortable little bungalow. Her healthy son…and now sons. Good friends, comforts and the man across the table.

Romance didn't exist. Love was often a one-way street. So where did that leave her? Wishing that the God she could no longer hear or feel would grant her a way out of this wedding?

Or was it possible that a marriage could work, if the wife and husband were friends and stayed that way? Without all the mess that went with romantic love, which was an impossible love?

"Help us to be ever thankful for Your blessings in our lives. Amen."

"Amen," Meg whispered out of habit, but she desperately hoped that God could hear her, even though she could not hear Him.

For if He could, then He would know her deepest wish, a prayer not for herself but for the little boys that

had brought her and Jared together. *Please, let it be different this time.* She wanted the twins to be happy. She
would sacrifice her newfound freedom for that end. But
it would be nice if, instead of love, there could be respect and friendship.

"Here. You get first crack at the noodles." Jared
pushed the carton across the table to her. "I have a few
rules that you're going to have to get used to. Ladies
first, when it comes to Thai food. Men first, when it
comes to pizza."

"Maybe I have a few rules, too."

"Bring them on." His smile was dazzling and as he
fixed his gaze on her, the look in his eyes said, "You can
trust me, Meg."

"If I cook, then you do the dishes."

"Ha, you think that's going to scare me? Honey, you
are looking at the best dish washer in the fine state of
Virginia."

"That I'll have to see to believe."

"I love a challenge." His gaze glittered as he dished
up a heaping serving of stir-fried beef. "Tomorrow's too
soon?"

"Way too soon."

"Next weekend?"

"Better."

Again, Jared felt that strange skittering of awareness he felt whenever God was working in his life. Unaware, Meg, graceful and elegant, daintily served up a
meager helping of chicken.

She moved like a symphony, like melody to his harmony, and he took in every detail. Her hair was braided
back in an elegant braid and the humidity had curled the
escaped tendrils that framed her porcelain face with

beauty. From the dainty gold bracelet dangling from her wrist, to the small stoned sapphire ring on her right hand, everything about her was soft, understated elegance and she was going to be his wife.

Never in his wildest dreams or in his lovesick teenager's imagination had he ever thought he'd have Meg for his fiancée. Meg Kierney. It had a perfect ring to it. And speaking of the perfect ring, he knew just where he would start on this new and challenging journey of making his bride fall in love with him.

Chapter Eight

Meg was parking beneath the neon brightness of the Starlight Diner's sign when she saw Rachel pull in a few spots down.

This was it. Her stomach took to quaking and she checked to make sure she'd turned off the minivan's headlights. She had. It was just nerves making her feel all jumbled and distracted. And the thought of telling Rachel about it was making her tremble.

There was no going back, no changing her mind, although she'd told no one. Jared had informed his mother, but she had to tell her mom over the phone. Her parents were in Florida for a last-minute cruise, and Sue Ellen had not been pleased with the news. Jared's family was not of the same social strata in Chestnut Grove, which mattered to her mom. Meg could already hear the arguments that would be made, when what mattered were the boys.

"Cake!" Luke demanded from his car seat and slapped the flat of his little hand on the tray. "Cake! Cake! Cake!"

"Ake!" Chance joined in, their voices identical and exceedingly loud.

Double the cute, double the volume. And double the love. Her battered heart seemed a little less torn. She set the brake, grabbed the diaper bag and climbed out into the night.

"Choc'lit cake. Yum." Luke sparkled like the precious blessing he was, looking as adorable as Chance.

"Yum." Chance seemed very impressed with this late evening outing. And also with her as she unbuckled him from his seat first. His fingers gripped her arms, and his hold on her was so tight he pinched her skin, but she didn't mind. His need tugged at her, this motherless little boy.

"Oh, I am in so much trouble." She took him in her arms, cherishing him, Luke's twin. She smoothed the cowlick on the back of his head, for all the good it did.

"Down! Down! Down!" Luke chanted, and Chance joined in. She managed to spring her son, locked up the van and capture each little boy by a sticky hand before Rachel ambled up.

"Oh, I have never seen anything more darling in my life." She knelt to get a better look at the twins. "Does this mean you and Jared have worked out a custody situation?"

"You might call it that. Come inside, let me treat you to dessert and we'll talk."

"This sounds serious." Rachel spoke over the boys' squeals of delight as they hopped up the walkway, first Luke, then Chance.

"Oh, what blessed little boys!" Sandra, in her tidy waitress uniform and apron, met them at the door. "Y'all are gonna need a booth and a couple of booster seats. Follow me."

"Choc'lit." Luke's wide eyes and grave tone imparted the importance of his visit.

"Choc'lit," Chance mimicked just as solemnly.

"I have just the thing, sweets. You sit down and mind your mama." Sandra left the menus on the edge of the table. "I'll get you some of those seats."

"Thank you." Meg let Luke climb into her lap.

"I get this one." Tenderly, Rachel plucked the other twin from the floor and into her arms. "How are you handling this?"

"I'm fine." It wasn't the truth, but it would be. Meg would make sure of it. Too much was at stake for it to be any other way. She kissed the top of Luke's head. "I need a favor."

"You want me to babysit? Any time."

"Thanks, but it's not that." *Just say it,* she told herself. She was already past the point of no return. "Jared and I have decided to get married. And I need—"

"Married?" Absolute shock was the only way to describe the look on Rachel's lovely face.

"It's the only way for the boys to grow up together. It's best for them." Meg did her best to sound positive. "It's not as though Jared and I are perfect strangers."

"No, you had that thing between you two in high school."

"It was nothing. Hardly a crush. Or a serious case of dislike. I never knew which." Before Rachel could read anything into that statement, Meg wanted to make it clear. "This isn't a real marriage. We're not in love. It makes sense for the boys."

"Yes, it does make good sense. Jared would make you a wonderful husband. I remember hearing his wife had died. I felt for him, since I'd lost Keith." Sadness filled Rachel's eyes when she spoke of her college sweetheart, but there was strength there, too. "Jared always was hardworking and kind. It doesn't seem as if those traits have altered one bit."

"That's what I'm banking on." Getting married sounded so sensible, a reasonable solution. It was, but her feelings were telling her something else. She swallowed, fighting them down, but it was like struggling against a deep river's current. "I would like you to be my maid of honor."

"Of course! I'd love nothing more."

Meg thanked her, grateful, but before she could say anything more, the waitress had returned with the booster seats. Meg welcomed the silence as they buckled the boys safely in. Sandra handed them crackers from her apron pocket.

It wasn't until after they'd ordered and the waitress had padded away before Meg said the most difficult words of all.

"I know this is last minute, but are you free on Saturday? We're getting married in the afternoon."

"*This* Saturday? Like in two days?"

"It's the only weekend that we had free between the two of us for a while."

"It's so sudden. Think of all that needs to be arranged."

"It's not like this is a real wedding."

"Meg! A wedding is a wedding. You can tell me whatever you wish, I know what's really going on. In high school it was that you two belonged together. I never quite understood how you two ended up going separate ways." Rachel studied her quietly for a moment before repeating, "A wedding is still a wedding. What do you need me to do? I have some time to help you plan and shop. We definitely need to go shopping."

"This is going to be a simple ceremony at the courthouse. I don't feel right having a big church wedding. I tried that, and it didn't work out so well." Shame burned her face and she stared at the tabletop. A shower of cracker crumbs sprayed her way.

She opened another packet from the pile Sandra had generously left on the corner of the table and handed each boy more crackers to destroy. "Besides, that would just make it look as though Jared and I were in love, and we're not. It's not like that."

"At least let me plan a few things."

"No, Rachel."

"What about a dress? Every bride needs something special for a wedding, practical or not."

"It's not a big deal." She couldn't let it be.

"Take my advice and don't expect so little. Take every happiness you can, because you never know until it's too late what you will regret. You deserve to be happy, and so do these adorable little guys."

As if in agreement, Chance stuffed the cracker into his mouth. Luke tossed his at the floor.

"If you expect too little, then you don't get hurt." Meg shocked herself by a rare confession. "If you expect everything and the moon, you're bound for disappointment."

"This is no fairy tale, this is your life. Make every moment the best you can."

Sandra arrived with fat slices of chocolate cake, meeting the boys' approval. Their delight changed the mood and the topic of conversation, but Rachel's words stayed in Meg's thoughts into the night. Where she sat watching a sickle moon in a bleak sky and wondered, was Jared awake and troubled, too?

"Hey, little guy, what's the matter?" Jared made his way through the shadows to the crib in the corner of Chance's room.

His son's sniffles came like sadness, low and desolate and lonely. The little boy was curled into a ball on his side, holding tight to his blanky, his thumb stuck in his mouth.

Big tears stood in his eyes. Chance had been subdued ever since they'd dropped by Meg's late with his first truckload of boxes. He wanted to move fast, get through the pain of it. Sort of the rip-off-the-bandage approach to moving. The less turmoil of a transition, the better for the boys and the better for the adults. Meg had a demanding career, and so did he, and on top of that she was certain enough their arrangement was going to be nothing but doom.

Well, he would show her there was no doom. Not a bit of it. He'd move in, get assimilated and they'd fall into a routine that worked for all of them.

"Hey, little man. You had a big day today. What's on your mind? Are you in deep thought?"

The tears in Chance's eyes got bigger. He stared soulfully over the curve of his fist.

"Did you like Meg taking care of you? I hear you and your brother got some chocolate cake."

"Eh." Chance pulled his blanket over his head.

So, he was already missing Meg and Luke?

Tonight, when Jared was finishing packing the last of the boxes in the roomy basement, he heard footsteps overhead. Meg had come home with the boys. She'd watched Chance for him so he could get a first load moved. He'd been missing all of them, so he hurried up and that's when he noticed both boys had the same exact blanket. Luke's was just as wash-worn and frayed as Chance's was.

Lord, You work in mysterious ways. I'm trusting that this is what You want for the twins. There was no answer save for the gentle rustle of the leaves outside the window.

"Come here, son." Jared gathered the small boy in his arms and nestled him against his chest. He eased into the rocking chair where Vanessa had spent so many hours rocking him as a new baby. It seemed as if her love lingered in this room, for some things were stronger than death.

"I think we found you a very nice new mom." He pressed a kiss against the crown of his son's head, letting the sweetness fill him up. Like starlight dusting the magnolia and oak standing guard outside, he felt the shadows of his worries slip away.

He realized suddenly with high definition clarity that God was giving him a new start. He was giving Chance a new mother. And maybe, he thought, remembering the stark sadness in Meg's soul, God was giving her a new start, too. They may be jumping the gun and leaping right into the middle of being a family together, but it was going to work out. They were going to fit.

Jared believed it. God worked in His own time, in His own way, a Father watching over His children.

He held his son long after Chance drifted off to sleep. He treasured the feel of his warm little body, weightless and seemingly boneless, slung against his chest. He savored the absolute trust as his son slept hard and deep.

The moonlight inched across the carpeted floor and finally out of the room, leaving only the dark glow of faint starshine and one man's hope. He was putting a lot of trust in a woman he hadn't known since high school. But he had faith.

I work hard, and when I walk through this door I'm hungry. Where's dinner? Eddie swore, using the Lord's name in vain, as he hurled his briefcase against the entry wall and the wham! echoed through the high-ceilinged foyer and through the cathedral ceilings of the upscale townhouse.

Meg jerked awake, feeling queasy and light-headed from a mild bout of the flu. The baby upstairs started to cry—loud, rhythmic squalls of agony. His earache was getting worse, in spite of a visit to the doctor. "I'm sorry, honey. I was stuck waiting to see the doctor—"

"Do you know the kind of day I've had?" Eddie's fury filled the house from foundation to rafters. "Get food on the table and shut that kid up. That screaming is giving me a headache—"

"Meg? Did you want me to order you something from the deli? I'm calling in an order for a bunch of us."

Meg startled, looking around, realizing that she'd been dreaming, that she must have fallen asleep sitting up in her chair. The bright glaze of the summer's sun was now splashing across her polished walnut desk and onto the framed photo of Luke.

She scrubbed the memory from her mind as she rubbed her eyes, focusing on her assistant standing in the doorway of her office. "No, thanks, Melissa. I've got errands to run."

"You were really lost in thought. Does it have anything to do with this gorgeous hunk of a man waiting outside to see you?"

Jared was here? Was it that time already? Sure enough, the luminous numbers on the clock on one of the bookcase shelves proclaimed it to be 3:30 p.m. How long had she been drowsing? It was a good thing the company's president hadn't dropped by for a chat and found one of his executives snoozing at her desk.

"Just send him in," she told her assistant. "And stop—I know what you're thinking."

"That it's been long enough since the divorce and it's time to start husband-hunting again? I say, good start."

With a wink, her naive assistant, who believed in fairy tales like marriage, slipped away. Suddenly there was Jared, filling the doorway, looking like a dream come true. No, she amended. He might seem like a dream, but dreams didn't exist. They ended come the light of day. She would rather have real, dependable and kind in a man any day.

"Wow, some place you've got here." He leaned one linebacker's shoulder against the doorjamb and looked around her digs. "You've done well for yourself. I always knew you would."

She shrugged. "I work hard, and I just happened into this position. It's been a good fit, and I love it here." She stood, smoothing her skirt and reaching for the earring that she'd taken off while she'd returned calls…before the impromptu nap.

"Nobody happens into anything. You look like you didn't sleep at all last night." He held out his big hand, palm up. His big masculine hand looked rugged and capable and strong. It was his tenderness she felt. His offer of friendship.

Her hand automatically lifted as if of its own accord, to rest on his. It seemed a long breathless moment as their gazes met and locked. The stock answer she intended to give him, about how she'd slept well enough, died on her tongue, for she knew he could see within her at that moment. The truth came out instead. "I didn't sleep at all."

"You're that worried about marrying me? Or marrying again at all? Or so soon after your divorce?"

"All of the above." She felt too vulnerable, as if she were revealing too much of herself. Pieces of herself that Jared could use against her. "I suppose it's different for men. They view wives differently."

"How so?"

"I don't know if men love the way women do."

"I'm sure they don't. Men love in a different way than women because they are men. God made us that way."

Meg's eyes clouded and her sorrow filled the air. "I can't go through that again, Jared. I—"

"I didn't mean that men were made to cheat. That is a disgrace to God. I mean that men are men. We're not so good at emotions, but I have a heart, just as you do. And a soul."

She closed her eyes briefly, as if in relief, as if in gratitude. When she opened them again, tears had gathered but did not fall.

Jared felt his chest cinch with affection. He wanted Meg to understand, so she would stop worrying, so she would stop hurting. "I loved Vanessa so much. Not to do my bidding and not to walk behind me, as I suspect your marriage was to Eddie, but beside me. That's all I want from you, Meg."

His fingers closed around her hand, so dainty and female. Her bones were small, her skin satin soft and he could smell the faint scent of her lotion. Something floral that made his eyes ache and his soul yearn for happiness with her. "I've said my piece. Now, what do you want in a husband?"

"I want someone who is kind and fair, who will help instead of hinder. I want to keep this life." She didn't know how to tell him all that she'd surrendered to Eddie, piece by piece, in the attempt to make their marriage better. "I'm so wrung out, Jared. I just can't—"

She didn't finish, but he felt her agony.

He hoped he could say the right words so she would believe in him. That they had a real chance together. "I won't lie and I won't betray your trust. In the ten years of my marriage, I never once considered breaking my vow to Vanessa. You have my word of honor. A vow I will swear to you and to God. I will never betray you. I will never willingly hurt you."

The strength in his words made her want to believe. "I think you are exactly what Luke needs. A good father."

It was all she could offer, but it seemed to be enough as a hint of a smile chased most of the lines of concern from Jared's handsome face.

"I hope I can be what *you* need, too," he said.

She couldn't answer because the emotion tangled like a knotted ball of yarn in her chest. She nodded, it was the best she could do, and held on tighter to Jared. With his hand covering hers, warm and capable, she breathed in some of his strength like the cool air. She felt better, knowing that out of all the men who could have adopted Luke's twin, it was Jared she was marry-

ing. Jared with whom she would be raising her son—
no, sons.

"Do you know what I really need?" she asked, the
honesty tumbling out of her and she could not draw it
back. "I really need a friend. A good friend. Not a husband to let me down. But a friend. Someone to count
on."

"Then you've got a friend." His fingers twined
through hers and held tight, as if he never intended to
let go. "For better of worse, for richer or poorer, I will
be right here for you."

"So will I." Relief spilled through her and she turned
away, letting go of him before he could see how deep
her fears went. And her scars. "I need my garment bag,
and then I'm ready."

"Then let's get married."

His arm slipped around her shoulders and they
walked together down the wide hall. Her heels clicked
on the marble floor and her reflection splashed in the
decorative mirrors and glass in the agency's impressive
entry. And for the first time she saw the image of her
and Jared walking together, side by side, as a couple.
As much as she tried to hold it back, hope lifted in her
soul.

*If You can hear me, Lord, please, help me to make
this work. For the boys' sake. For Jared's. And,* she
added, *for mine.*

Sandra Lange had a long day. Days tended to be
very long when you spent them on your feet serving
folks. She'd started breakfast prep before 6:00 a.m. and
it was nine forty-five at night and she was still here. Exhausted as she was, there was no better place for her to

be. No one was at home waiting for her. All she had was this diner, and she was thankful to the good Lord for it, but there were nights when it wasn't close to being enough.

She knew what was troubling her. Meg Kierney's little boys. They were adopted, and seeing their sweet little faces reminded her of all her mistakes. Of all that should have been different if she hadn't been so young and needed a man's love and approval so badly. A man who wasn't worthy of her trust.

Gerald Morrow had destroyed her life thirty-five years ago. But she was not afraid of him. Not anymore.

She made sure the doors were locked first, in case a late-night customer spotted her lights on, before she dialed the phone. Nerves had her heartbeat racing, but she was ready to hear his voice. She was ready for his insults.

She didn't have to wait long—he answered on the third ring.

"Mayor Morrow."

"Gerald." She waited for him to recognize her voice. "I bet you never thought you'd near from me again, did you?"

"Sandra. No, I no longer associate with lowly waitresses."

She let his insult roll off her shoulders. She was not here to bicker or win an argument, not with the image of those adorable little twins in her mind's eye. Adopted twins. "You don't scare me one bit. Not anymore. You tell me what happened to my baby. I want to find him."

"I don't know what you're talking about." Glibly, he lied like the rat that he was. "Do not call me again."

The line went dead.

That was supposed to stop her? Recently she'd buried her father, she'd been diagnosed with breast cancer and she was utterly alone. There had been no husband or children after her affair with Gerald. Tears welled hot and bitter even after thirty-five years. Her arms still ached for her child—she didn't even know if he'd been a boy or a girl.

A baby Gerald had made her sign away when she'd been groggy and confused after a complicated birth and an emergency hysterectomy. The surgery had saved her life, but Gerald had taken it in another way that day. She'd trusted him, trusted his promise that he'd leave his wife for her and their baby. But he'd betrayed her with one lie after another. He'd stolen her child, the only child she could ever have.

Her baby would be thirty-four years old. She could never put this agony down until she knew what had happened to him. Had he or she grown up happy and loved? Was he now married with children? Visions of grandchildren, of being a part of a real family again, taunted her. Regrets weighed on her soul.

She hit redial. She didn't expect Gerald to answer. Fine, the weasel. He could hide from his crimes, but she was determined. At the beep following his voice mail message, she made her intentions clear. "I'm going to find our baby. You won't help me, fine. I'll find someone who can. The truth will come out one way or another, so beware."

She was shaking when she hung up. Not from fear or rage, but from relief. Her life kept passing by, the days spilling like water downstream, and she was fifty-five. That was a long time to keep a secret. It was a long time to yearn for a precious baby stolen from her arms.

She felt the tides of her life begin to change as she flipped open the yellow pages and went in search of a private investigator.

Chapter Nine

"Oh, you look beautiful," Rachel breathed as she reached up to fuss with the spray of freesia she'd tucked into Meg's hair. "Your groom will be too dazzled to speak."

"You're being kind, but I appreciate it." Meg studied her reflection in the small mirror tacked above the row of sinks in the courthouse women's restroom.

Her cheeks were too red from nerves. Her eyes too bright. Her forehead too furrowed. Maybe she ought to haul out her makeup bag, but no, Jared was waiting and no amount of cover-up was going to make walking down the hallway any easier.

"You've got something old and blue." Rachel pointed out the sapphire drop necklace, which had been a high school graduation gift from Rachel. "I'm glad you still have it after all these years."

"I treasure it." Fondly, Meg touched the dainty sapphire with her fingertips. Friendship. That was something that lasted, something she could count on. "And my dress is new. Thanks for helping me pick it out."

"You know how I dislike shopping." Rachel's hazel eyes twinkled. She looked stunning as always in a tailored designer jacket and skirt, and she looked like a model with her hair swept up off her long neck. "I have one more surprise. Here, you need something borrowed. This bracelet goes with your dress."

"It's far too expensive and brand-new. I can't. I'd be afraid of losing it."

"Nonsense. You borrow it now, and keep it for good memories of today." Rachel removed the delicate gold and platinum bracelet from her slender wrist and clipped it on Meg's.

"You thought of everything." Meg's mind had been a whirl since Jared had dropped her back at her office after picking up the marriage license. "I hope you know how important you are to me. You are a wonderful person and a great friend."

"Although you never let on, I could see you didn't have a good marriage before. I hope this second time with Jared brings you every kind of happiness."

That seemed far too much to ask for. Meg concentrated on what was important. What was attainable. "He's a good man. He'll be a good father."

"You look shaky. Here, do you want to sit down?"

"No, I want to run." Meg took a steadying breath. "I'm ready. Having you here means a lot. I don't know why I'm so nervous. This is just an arrangement for the boys."

"Of course." Rachel's face had a knowing look as she gathered her small tailored pocketbook and slipped the strap over her slim shoulder. As if maybe she suspected there was much more to the sudden marriage. "Do you have Jared's ring?"

"His mom said she would take care of it. He and Vanessa had matching bands, so she kept his dad's wedding ring all these years for him." Meg had appreciated Donna's thoughtfulness. "Eddie's family were never a part of our lives. A kind and loving mother-in-law. She's going to be a welcome change."

"Why wouldn't Donna love you? She is getting the best daughter-in-law that a woman could ask for." Rachel took Meg by the hand and opened the restroom door. "Are you ready?"

No. Then she thought of Luke and Chance, and the fear slid into the background. "I'm ready."

It wasn't easy taking the first steps. Her heels clicked on the tile and echoed on the long high walls. The rush and din from the offices and activity inside the old, cavernous building didn't seem loud enough to cover up the wild thumping of her pulse.

And then there was Jared, standing as she entered the room. "Just in time," he said easily. "We're next."

"Mama!" Luke welcomed, holding on tight to Donna.

"Mm-mmma!" Chance seconded as he gripped Luke's hand.

The boys gave her the opportunity she needed to turn away from Jared before he could see how hard this was for her. He looked so calm and certain, she didn't want him to see on her face exactly how much she didn't want this wedding. She knelt until she was eye level with the twins, who were dressed in matching shirts and pants. "Hey, my good boys. You're looking awfully handsome. Donna, did you do this?"

"It's my credit card's fault. It just leaped out of my purse and bought those two little outfits. And since I brought my camera, I thought we would take a few photos. Do you want to sit right down there? Jared? Come over here, son." Donna produced her new digital camera and squinted at the controls, muttering about new-fangled contraptions.

"Let me take the pictures, Mrs. Kierney." Rachel deftly handled the expensive camera. "I'm honored to take your first picture as a family."

As a family. Jared felt his soul move like a slow powerful riptide yanking him out from shore. He didn't understand it, but he wasn't afraid. The best stuff of life was also the scariest. Because there was so much to lose. He knew exactly how much. It wasn't easy opening his heart to the moment. Once, he'd been leveled by grief. He never wanted to feel that way again. But that was the price of loving.

He watched, wrestling with his emotions, while Meg abandoned her chair and helped his mother into it. *She's a good woman,* he thought. *I know she'll be a wonderful wife.* Already, he was falling in love with her, and he calmly stood behind his mom, laid his hand on her shoulder and gestured for Meg at his side.

I'm willing to take the good moments of life, Father. I'm giving up my fears to You. God knew best, and Jared felt deeply reassured as he put his arm around Meg. He could feel her tension. He ached for her and leaned close. It felt like the most natural thing in the world to whisper in her ear. "I'm a very blessed man, getting to marry you. I just want you to know that."

Her eyes met his and he could see the well of emotion. His words mattered to her. *He* mattered to her. His chest filled with peace and he forgot where they were, or that there were people surrounding them. All he saw was his beautiful, gentle Meg.

"Chance and Luke! Look up here!" Rachel drew the twins' attention and the flash strobed. "Wait! Let me take another one just in case someone blinked."

"I don't know if I can keep them in place much longer." Donna chuckled as she gripped each twin by the shoulder.

The flash blinded them again, and the door to the judge's chamber opened. A young couple that didn't look a day over twenty emerged, the bride glowing with radiant joy. The newlyweds held hands as they strolled away, hardly seeing anything or anyone for the way they could not take their eyes from the other.

Meg ached, torn between hoping that the young bride would find marriage to be everything she imagined, everything to keep that joy in her heart, and afraid she would not. That she might discover that joy was a fleeting thing. That vows could be more like shackles. That a man who vowed to love and honor might not.

It was a good thing she wasn't marrying for love, Meg thought. She was older, wiser, more experienced. As the clerk motioned them in and asked for their paperwork, she felt stronger knowing this marriage was based on something real, commitment to the most precious blessings on earth: their sons.

So she was certain as Jared took her by both hands. Forthright as she repeated her vows to honor and cherish, and committed her life to Jared's. She slipped the plain gold band that Donna had brought on Jared's finger, sealing her promise.

She was surprised when Jared pulled a ring from his jacket pocket and slid its cool smoothness onto her finger. His words were as true as the diamonds shimmering in a slim, exquisite band.

"Until death do us part, Meg, I will be your best friend," he whispered as the judge declared them married.

Friends. That was why this felt exactly right as Jared cupped her chin in the palm of his hand. His lips hovered over hers for a brief moment and, gaze to gaze, she felt him in her soul like a breeze on her skin. Then his mouth slanted over hers and his kiss was tender. Before she could let her eyelids drift shut, he broke the kiss and was moving away, leaving her reeling. With any luck, he would not kiss her again.

The judge congratulated them, and Rachel chased after the twins, who were heading for the door the clerk had opened. Luke led the way into the hall followed by his shadow, Chance, with Gramma close behind.

"I'll just be keeping these two precious babies for the night." Donna sparkled with mischief as she took a firm hold of Luke. "Newlyweds need their private time to celebrate. You come get them anytime. I'd keep them forever otherwise."

Celebrate? Meg had heard Donna's words, but she couldn't digest them. They didn't make sense to her. She and Jared didn't need to *celebrate,* as Donna called it. Didn't Jared tell his mother that this was not a real marriage?

"It will give me some time to spend with my grandsons." Donna looked so happy as she began telling the boys what she had planned for them. Hotdogs on the grill and cake for dessert.

"Cake! Cake! Cake!" The boys chanted, their voices echoing down the hallway despite Donna's attempts to quiet them.

Clearly charmed, the happy grandmother called over her shoulder, "You newlyweds have a lovely evening."

Meg was at a loss. "You can't let her think we're going to—"

"This marriage is real enough. Just like my respect for you. Like the vows I made to you. We're not like those newlyweds that floated out of here desperately in love, but what we have together isn't a small thing."

His hand found hers and he traced the beautiful ring he'd given her. "You're my wife, now. I'm your husband. We're a team. That's what a marriage is, right?"

He could say the right thing to quiet her fears.

"Let's head home. We'll order in something. I was hoping to get a load moved before dark. It's not the most romantic way to spend a wedding night."

"But it sounds right to me." There was so much to do and limited time. "I'll come help you. I have some empty boxes in the basement I can donate to the cause."

They were a team. *That* felt right. *That* was something she could get excited about. He kept hold of her hand as they hurried down the hall and into the bright radiance of the summer sun.

"What sounds good for dinner?" Jared asked as he pulled his pickup to a stop against the curb. Shade from the oaks sprinkled over them as he killed the engine. "Your pick."

"Mine? Eddie was never so generous after putting a ring on my finger."

"Pardon me for saying so, but Eddie must be the dumbest man alive if he treated you that way. He obviously doesn't know what's important. I do."

"You are too good to be true, Jared Kierney, but I like it. I love the lasagna at the little Italian place on the River Walk."

"I've got a thing for their rigatoni." He popped out into the heat of the late afternoon, and circled around the hood to help her down from the truck.

It was such a gentlemanly gesture, and it touched her. What a nice man. This friendship idea was a great one. They would keep their hearts safe, they would avoid all that messy needing and loving and disappointing. She let him take her hand, and their strides matched as they headed down the walkway.

"If you want to call in the order," she proposed, "I'll go dig my empty boxes out of the basement."

"Deal." He skipped up the stairs to open the screen door for her. The inner door, which was supposed to be locked, opened to reveal a beautifully printed banner proclaiming in pink and blue scroll Congratulations, Meg and Jared! The silver, blue and gold balloons floating in bouquets at either end had wedding bells in black ink printed on them. Shimmery ribbons fluttered and a half dozen voices shouted out, "Congratulations!"

"Why didn't you announce that you were getting married?" Pilar was dressed for a party.

Meg could only stare. There were people in her house. Not just any people—her closest friends.

"You could have mentioned it at brunch on Sunday." Anne stepped forward, but she was smiling too brightly to seem upset with being left out of the loop. "Did you think you could get away with keeping this quiet?"

"Especially not when I have a key," Rachel added.

Meg surveyed the faces of her friends, seemingly so happy for her, and finally, there was Rachel, who had to have arranged this. "I love you all, but you shouldn't have gone to this trouble." *Because this marriage isn't what you think.*

Jared's hand settled on the curve of her shoulder, and she knew she wasn't alone trying to explain. Or in trying to figure out what to say.

"Ben, Ramon, Jonah." Jared's warm baritone rumbled through her. "Meg and I are blown away by this."

Two of the men Meg recognized from the church she used to attend seemed to be nice enough, including Jonah, the reverend's son. And there was Pilar's brother Ramon, a familiar face. Friendly, not uptight, the way Eddie's friends had been. Maybe that was another sign this marriage was going to work out all right.

"We couldn't believe you took the plunge, man." Ramon winked before presenting two champagne flutes full of bubbling liquid.

Meg accepted the glass, although she didn't drink. Then she recognized the scent of sparkling juice. His friends had come and so had hers in celebration of what should be a happy event.

"Meg was mean and made me marry her." Jared winked and everyone laughed, recognizing the joke for what it was. "Seriously, I consider myself privileged to have such a beautiful and amazing wife. I'm surprised she would agree to have me."

Sincere respect. The power of it touched her like nothing else could. Already this marriage was different. Eddie had hated her work, and found fault with her at every turn.

Jared was not a man who would ever intentionally hurt her. She couldn't begin to measure the relief as it lifted from her spirit like the bubbles in the glass. This wasn't the evening she'd planned to spend with him. As their wedding ceremony had been, their wedding night may as well be a practical one, too.

But as her friends and Jared's friends led them into the house, she realized this was fine, too. The dining room table was set with her best china and lace cloths. The silver candelabra was loaded with lit, pastel candles that glowed with warmth. The warm scents filled the air of Southern cooking—rich gravy and baked beans, ribs, chicken-fried chicken, mashed potatoes, butter beans and sweet potato pie. Gifts were gaily wrapped and stacked on the top of the buffet.

As the doorbell rang and the rest of Jared's Bible Study members arrived with desserts and gifts and good wishes and invitations for her to join them at their next meeting.

"Is this better than what we had planned?" Jared pulled her aside and leaned close to ask her.

"It is. This is your home now, too, and all this, seeing both sets of our friends here, makes it official. "

"Yes. This is *our* home." He put his arm around her.

The way any friend would do to another in a moment of emotional closeness. At least that's what Meg told herself. So, why did his nearness make her remember his tender kiss?

"The newlyweds dish up first." Pilar took charge, heading toward the kitchen. "We'll do food, then presents, then dessert."

"After you, my wife." As gallant as a knight of old, Jared put her first. He carried her plate and made sure she had dished up enough food. He held her chair for her. He didn't take his sparkling eyes off her. He was man enough to make even a woman like her hope that this convenient marriage could be a happy one.

After the delicious dinner was consumed and the presents opened, Rachel tapped the edge of her goblet.

The lively conversations quieted so she could speak. "It's time for dessert. Anne suggested we move everyone into the living room, and we'll serve you in there. And while you're waiting, Meg and Jared may as well start opening the two last gifts we held back."

"You are far too generous," Meg answered, amazed.

Jared felt no small amount of pride watching his wife. She was gracious and classy—he liked that about her—but sincere. A rare combination. He thought Vanessa would approve of his choice of a mom for Chance.

It wasn't about forgetting her or finding a replacement for her, because true love was never-ending. Nor was it about moving on, because grieving over Vanessa had been the hardest job of his life. He would never put her loss behind him like something to get over. A person shouldn't get over love, but carry it with him.

He wasn't replacing her. He was simply living. Because he'd loved Vanessa, he was here today, surrounded by all these terrific people. Married to a woman who stirred his soul, when it had been still and silent for so long. He was a blessed man.

He'd zoned out, and missed whatever it was Meg had said to make everyone laugh. In her quiet way, she was laughing, too. Alight and sparkling and although she was a woman of education and means and accomplishment, he could see that glimmer of the young Meg he'd known so well, full of fire and innocence.

It felt natural to take his place at her side on the couch. Pilar called Anne and Rachel from the kitchen, deciding to give their combined gifts as a threesome. Meg chose to open the smallest one first, and inside the wrapping paper was a scrapbook.

When Meg opened the first page, there were moments

from each of the boys. A snapshot of Chance in his incubator. A Polaroid of Luke cradled in Meg's arms, leaving the hospital. A picture of Luke crawling for the first time. Another of Vanessa with Chance tucked in her arms, holding his bottle. Each page was filled with the images and memories of the boys, together for the first time. Rachel, Pilar and Anne had to have spent long hours on this.

"I get that you had my mom's help in this," he finally said. "But how did you do this without Meg knowing?"

"Her mom said the maid could let me in, so I could help myself to the pictures she had and copy what we needed. Plus, between us, we had some photos to donate," Anne volunteered.

"And we left the last few pages blank, for you to complete together," Pilar added. "There's another present to open."

Overcome, unable to speak, Meg peeled back the tape at the corner of the large awkward gift, that was obviously a large picture frame. As she tore the paper away, her jaw dropped as she studied the collage picture frame. "Oh, you didn't! How am I ever going to thank you three enough for all this?"

"You can thank us best by being happy," Rachel answered.

Meg wiped at the tears blurring her eyes, as she studied one image after another. Individual pictures of the twins from birth to walking, from infant to toddler.

"What struck us the most is that the boys are almost identical, not only in looks but also to the gestures in the photos and in their clothes," Anne informed them.

"It's true." Meg leaned forward to study the pictures, her soft red hair tumbling over her slender shoulder. She brushed the lock unconsciously behind her ear, a simple gesture, one she did all the time without noticing she was doing it. He could not take his gaze away from her fluid movements.

"We're truly a family now." He scooted closer, so he was pressed against her side, and he could feel the soft wisps of her hair feather against his jaw. Then he saw the center picture—the photo Rachel had taken outside the judge's chambers this afternoon. The one with his mother sitting in the middle, aglow with happiness and her twin grandsons standing before her. Her hands were on each of their little shoulders, holding them still. He and Meg were behind her, side by side. Your first family picture, Rachel had said at the time. She must have raced back here, used one of those nifty photo printers, and finished the frame and wrapped it, hurrying all the while.

"The other gifts are duplicates of the pictures we used," Rachel explained as she knelt to cover Meg's hand with hers.

Through all the gifts they opened and the delicious black forest cake from the local bakery and good fellowship, Jared couldn't get the pictures out of his head. While Meg went to help her friends with the dishes, and they protested mightily, he went in search of a hammer.

With Meg's advice, he hung the picture in the living room above the mantel. He took the mirror that had been there up to Meg's bedroom, as she'd asked. Separate beds, separate rooms.

The emotion hit him. He wanted this to be a whole marriage. That unwavering bond of souls, the soft cushion of companionship, that simpatico comfort of knowing that every day was the best day because he was spending it with his wife.

He saw now why God had brought him here. Why

He'd separated the boys at birth. Why of all the women to have adopted Chance's twin, He'd chosen Meg. Why He'd found a way to heal the brutal tides that this earthly life and choices made by Eddie Talbot had brought to him and to Meg. God demonstrated that healing happened everyday. Moved beyond words, Jared returned to the party, grateful for this new blessing of true love in his life.

Chapter Ten

The small group left early. It wasn't even eight o'clock. Meg blushed when she heard one of the men comment that it was their wedding night, and time for the newlyweds to be left alone. She caught hold of her three dearest friends on the porch, before they could slip away with the same excuse. "I don't know how you managed to do all of this, but thank you so much. You have no idea how much it means."

"I think we might." Rachel hugged her first. "I wish you great happiness, my friend."

"And more happiness." Anne was next to offer a hug.

"Every happiness," Pilar finished, giving the last hug.

Meg waved as her friends departed. Friends who had worked long hours to make this evening special. They each climbed into their respective cars and zipped away in the lengthening shadows.

Jared came up behind her on the walkway. Mercy gave a "meow" as she hiked across the grass, returning to the house now that all those—in her view—unwelcome people had finally left.

"You look exhausted." His big hand snaked beneath her hair and cupped her nape. "You're all knotted up tight. Want me to rub this out for you?" He gave a comforting stroke.

Meg felt her vertebrae sigh. "Maybe that's not such a good idea. Are you still going to get a load tonight?"

"No. I'm beat. I'm just going to grab my overnight bag from the truck and be in." He abandoned his hold on her, jangled the keys in his free hand and took off down the walkway.

His overnight bag? He was staying? Meg watched as he tugged an athletic bag out from the seat on the club cab. He locked up with a chirp from his remote and the lights flashed.

Sure enough, her eyes weren't deceiving her. Jared shouldered the strap, as confident as always. "I took that mirror up to your room, but I didn't know where you wanted it. If you want me to hang it before I collapse, say so now. Because if I sit down, I probably won't be able to get back up."

"Me, too." Meg stifled a yawn, although she had quite a few chores left to do in her evening routine. Plants and flowers to water. The bird feeders to fill. The cats to feed. The garbage to take out. The list went on in her head. "I'll worry about the mirror tomorrow."

"Good enough. Do you mind if I watch a little TV? I want to catch the baseball scores."

"Sure."

Marriage with Jared so far was pretty nice. Friendship, that was the secret. She'd been up all night last night worrying how today would go. She hadn't expected such a good day.

Grateful, she headed to the kitchen for her first

stop—feeding the cats, who did not appreciate having their routines disrupted with so many people in their house. She fed them a little extra and made sure she plied them with a few kitty treats before moving into the backyard.

The automatic sprinkler system and the drip beds watered the entire yard, but she had a fondness for potted flowers spilling everywhere on the patio. She watered the big clay pots, the window boxes and the honeysuckle climbing the back porch rails and trellis. As she worked, hummingbirds hovered overhead to stare at her with clear urgency. She looked up to see the feeders were definitely empty.

"All right, I'll do that next." Meg wound up the hose and found Jared watching her.

"Do you always talk to the birds?"

"Well, they communicate, I communicate." Her hands were wet from the nozzle and she flicked the wetness from her fingertips. "I thought you were going to be a couch potato and watch sports."

"Yeah, but I wanted some iced tea first, and I spotted you through the windows. I thought you were going to wind down, not do more chores, or I would have offered to help."

"I've got it covered."

"It's going to take me a while to figure out your routines and how to fit in. When to help out." He produced a pitcher of liquid. "I found this next to the iced tea. Hummingbird food?"

"Yes."

"Then let me be useful. I'll get it, short stuff."

"Hey, I'm not that short. I'm above average for a woman."

"Sure, but you're petite to me." Confident at his over six-foot height, he grinned down at her as he gently nudged her aside, reached over her head and easily unhooked the feeder.

"Aren't you handy?" It was easier to say that instead of what she really felt. That he would help her, that he would think to help was amazing. Holding back her feelings, she took the empty feeder from him and removed the top so he could fill it.

One of the hummingbirds returned to hover in front of her, chirping as if to say, "Hurry, my babies are hungry."

On the porch rail, Goodness flicked her tail and dreamed.

"I miss the boys," she said suddenly.

The second feeder clunked to rest on the table beside her and there was Jared, taking the full feeder from her. "I miss them, too. They sort of grow on you."

"Just the tiniest bit." She uncapped the empty feeder and listened to Jared's easygoing steps pad away from her. And yet he felt so close, as if he were standing beside her.

She struggled to snap off the stubborn plastic top with the yellow flowers. "It's funny how Luke can run me ragged. And yet, when I'm away from him, I'm just lonely for him."

"I know." Jared stepped away, saying nothing more, as the hummingbird buzzed him as if to order him back, and then began to feed. "Let me hang that one, too."

She let him, and snapped the top on the pitcher, made sure the hose water was off and patio furniture cushions were all picked up and stowed—they were.

"Any more chores for the night?" Jared asked. "I

took the garbage out earlier and even put a new sack in the trash can."

"Wow. I'm impressed."

"That's the idea. Are you going to come in, or spend some time alone?" He seemed to be able to sense how she was feeling, that she needed some space.

"That would be great. Thanks, Jared."

"Any time, pretty lady. Now it's me, a glass of iced tea and *Sports Center*." He padded into the house. The door clicked, and she was alone.

She locked up and set the alarm. She noticed Jared wasn't in the living room. The TV was off. Maybe he'd gotten tired and decided to make up the bed in the third bedroom she used as an office but had decided to surrender to him. There was a love seat that pulled out into a bed, and she was sure the double-sized sheets were clean and folded and in the linen closet—

She skidded to a stop at the last doorway down the hall. It looked as if he'd settled in somewhat. The light was on. Voices were coming from the little TV in the corner. Running water came from the partially shut bathroom door across the hall.

The bathroom door opened and there was Jared without a shirt and a toothbrush in hand. "Hey. Is the TV too loud?"

"No. I just came to say good-night."

"I noticed you have a nice roomy bedroom and a bigger TV. I wouldn't mind moving."

"You're having fun with this, aren't you? You're smiling."

"No, I'm not." His grin went a little wider. "We're married, you know. I just thought sometime." He shrugged.

"You know this wasn't our deal." She wanted to scold him, but how could she when he was looking so charming and obviously enjoying the gentle kidding. She was intrigued, and that was no way to be. What on earth was wrong with her? "I brought fresh sheets. Let me make up the bed."

"I can do that. You know they call it the master bedroom, right?" He didn't look sorry as he began removing the cushions from the love seat. "I'm the master of the house."

"Then I'm master, too—well, I don't want to use the word 'mistress.' You said we were on equal footing here." She set the sheets on the edge of the desk and went to help him draw out the folding mattress and frame. "I know what you're trying to do."

"That's the problem with marrying an educated woman. They think they are so smart." With a wink, Jared rolled his eyes.

She laughed. "You can be as charming as you want, it's never going to make a bit of difference."

"That's why your eyes are sparkling." He grabbed the bottom sheet and unfolded it with a snap. "This is a real marriage, you know that, right? I care about you, Meg."

Her heart stopped pumping and the blood rushed from her head. She knew Jared was talking about this lightly, but he was letting her know. He was changing the agreement and that wasn't fair. She remembered his kiss at the ceremony. "I'm not ready for intimacy."

"We're just doing this a little backward is all. We put the wedding before the dating and the courting and the romance. We got that marriage thing out of the way. And now you can just relax and let me date you."

"Married people don't date."

"Maybe they should." He tucked in the corners on his side of the bed. "Are you going to make me say it?"

"Say what?"

"The truth."

"Maybe I don't want the truth, either." She took refuge in shaking out the folded top sheet and figuring which was the top and which was the bottom edge. She watched him through her lashes. He still hadn't put a shirt back on and his skin was bronzed from the sun and emphasized his muscular arms, pecs and abdomen. Stop looking at him, she thought.

"I have been without Vanessa for almost two years. I don't know about you, but I've never gotten used to sleeping alone."

"No, me either."

"I miss the comfort. I miss knowing that I'm safe as can be beside the person I trust the most. I miss knowing I'm not alone. That's all I'm asking for whenever you're ready, Meg. As for intimacy, I'd sure like that, too, but again, I want you to be ready. I want you to sure. I want you to love me in return."

He appeared so big and powerful and yet he was showing her where he was most vulnerable. That he needed her to love him. *Already I'm failing him.* She felt ancient and wrung out.

Eddie had taken so much from her. Some nights it felt as if he'd taken everything inside her. Jared watched her with wide, measuring eyes, his body language relaxed and not wary.

"I don't think I can ever trust a man like that again."

She wanted Jared to know the truth. "I was sort of hoping we would be like roommates. You know, your life and my life are separate. Separate money. Separate decisions. Separate beds."

"I see." A muscle ticked in his jaw, but it was the only sign he was displeased. "And this friendship thing?"

She'd hurt him. She could feel the sting of it like a slap to her cheek. It wasn't what she wanted. "Our lives are going to intersect, of course. Living in the same house. Raising our boys. Doing the work that needs doing around here."

"I know you don't mean that as coolly as you say it. We have to figure this out, Meg. I've lost my heart once. I don't want to do it again, but I'm willing to risk loving you." He cupped her face with his big rugged hand. "What about you?"

She so longed to give in to the comfort of his touch. To close her eyes and melt against his warm palm and let him draw her against his strong chest. To let all her worries and all her lessons learned and all her defenses drift away like a leaf on the wind. But that was a trap she'd fallen into once. Never again.

She stood tall, and instead of turning to him, she faced away. "I like what we have agreed to, Jared. Friendship is a lot stronger and lasts longer. I can't do anything more than that."

"I'll wait. I'm not in a rush, but I want more."

"And I don't." Her throat burned, because she could see how seeing the gift of the boys' pictures had affected him. The colorful photographs, when put together like that, made them look like a real family. The kind of illusion she used to wish for with all her heart, as a teen-aged girl. The kind of dream she'd held in her soul when she'd been a college girl working hard to succeed, and falling in love with Eddie.

Wishes and dreams were like the balloons downstairs, suspended in midair for as long as the helium stayed. But inevitably they deflated and fell to the ground.

"I'll get the boxes out in the morning," she said gently, because she did care about him. More than she wanted to admit. More than she thought was wise. "Good night, Jared."

She eased the door closed behind her, and sank into the dark shadows in the hallway. The house seemed to echo around her as she made her way down the hall to make sure the doors were locked against the coming night.

The sun had sank low beneath the trees, casting shade everywhere, bleeding colors from the yard and house, and leaving the sky a bold blue. Her gaze was drawn toward the brilliant color, as if seeking God. But there was no one there.

Morning dawned, and the first streaks of golden light found Meg on her porch, savoring her first cup of Earl Grey tea. Shirley sat on the cushion beside her, enjoying the morning before the heat hit. Spray from the sprinklers misted over them, and Meg loved the coolness on her face.

It had been strange waking up to know Jared was in the same house, just down the hall. She'd thought he was sleeping—she hadn't heard him get up—until she found the note left in the center of the kitchen counter. *Went out to hunt and gather.*

She'd rubbed her fingertips over his jaunty scrawl. Confident and forthright, the way Jared had always been. Those days as rivals on the high-school newspaper were over. And now they had to find a way to make this work. While she'd made her tea and fed the cats, she couldn't get his words out of her thoughts. *This is going to be a real marriage.*

No, it wasn't. It would be real in the sense that it was legal. They'd taken vows which she fully intended to keep. But she had no heart left to give. Couldn't he feel that? And how could he have any heart, either, after losing his wife?

She wasn't about to risk the boys' happiness over something as impossible to attain as romantic love. Jared would come to understand that in time. She took another sip of tea, savoring the sugar that had fallen to the bottom of the cup. It was moving day, for better or worse, and this was likely the only moment to herself she would be able to find.

As if on cue, Jared's pickup pulled up into the driveway. The tinted windows hid him from her view, but she could hear the faint bass of a popular Christian band. The door opened and she wasn't prepared for the leap of her spirit. It was as if sunlight had first shone into her world.

Shirley gave a flick of her tail. She did not appreciate the change in her morning routine and hopped down, sauntering across the porch and retreating into the air-conditioned house through her kitty door. Goodness and Mercy, huddled in the shade in the corner, scurried after her. What was with the cats? Meg had to lean over in the swing, which shook and swayed with her movement, to better see around the corner of the house.

There was Jared, with the pickup door wide open. "C'mon, would ya?" He seemed to be speaking to someone just beyond her range of sight. He hadn't gotten the boys yet, had he?

A brown streak zinged out from behind the SUV and arrowed through the sprinklers. It skidded to a stop right in front of the nozzle. Meg blinked, unable to believe her eyes. What was a big brown dog doing in her yard? Drenched by the sprinkler, the canine opened his doggy mouth and his big pink tongue lolled out. He seemed to be smiling.

"Buster, get over here!" Jared kept his voice low, because it was early and the neighborhood was likely more asleep than awake, and the chocolate lab took advantage of it by pretending he didn't hear. "Buster. Heel."

The dog turned to let his other side be pelted by the jets from the sprinkler head. So this was Jared's dog? How had he described his pet? As big and dopey?

"I'm not coming in there after you." Jared shut the door and circled around the lawn, and Meg lost sight of him around the corner of the house.

He reappeared along the edge of the porch, carrying something in his arm like a football. He looked good this morning, with his hair still damp from the shower. She hadn't heard him use the bathtub in the main bathroom, either.

He must have spotted her when he drove up because he turned toward her, bounding up the steps, wearing light summer clothes—a pair of short and an athletic tank. The package he'd protected from the sprinklers was a white baker's box, from one of the best bakeries along the River Walk. "I hope you still love doughnuts."

"No, I hate them. Absolutely. Positively." She groaned, even as her mouth watered. "They're like a thousand calories each, mostly calories from fat. And they are addictive. Whoever invented doughnuts is a very bad person."

"My sentiments exactly. It's a shame I have custard-filled ones, but I'll just take them inside and eat 'em myself. They're even chocolate-covered."

"I will not be tempted."

"That's too bad." He settled into the swing next to her, the chains creaking pleasantly with his added weight. "It's nice some things never change. I still know your favorite doughnut."

"You remembered that from your high school nemesis?"

"You'd be surprised what I noticed about you."

"I thought I annoyed you back then."

"No, not at all. How could anyone so lovely and smart be annoying? Difficult to beat at tests and G.P.A., sure, but I always liked you." He opened the box and offered her first pick.

The incredibly sweet scent of rich chocolate topping and doughy doughnut filled the air. "Okay, I'll only have one."

"Good. Then my peace offering is a success."

She concentrated on taking the plump, gooey pastry. Last night stood like a great wall between them, and she didn't want to talk about it. The chocolate was sticky and melted on her tongue. The pastry was light as air. The custard rich and creamy, and she sighed. "Perfection."

"Good." Jared bit into the end of a maple bar and put the box on the cushion between them. "What do you think about my dog?"

"Does he always do that?"

"Yep."

The streams of spray from the sprinklers began to hiss and diminish. The leggy chocolate Lab looked devastated, then realized the side yard sprinklers were turning on. He took off, tongue hanging, and disappeared in the direction of the spurting sprinkler heads.

"He can't go far. There's a fence between the houses."

"He never runs off. He would never want to go too far away from the place that gives him food and puppy treats." Jared took another bite of his gooey doughnut. "He's housebroken, he's great with kids and he likes cats."

"As long as he leaves my flowers and rose bushes alone, he and I will get along all right."

"Good. About last night—"

"I don't want to go there," she interrupted him and stood. "We have a lot to do today. I'll go make another pot of tea before we go to your place and start filling boxes."

Jared watched her go, moving with the summer's breeze in her long, thick hair. Taking his heart with her as she disappeared from his sight, leaving him alone.

As he finished his maple bar, he had to consider the fact that this marriage might not be so easy. And that Meg might fight him every step of the way.

Chapter Eleven

Panic was building. She didn't love Jared, she wasn't going to love Jared, and she would never allow herself to love him. Meg darted through her living room, making the windows rattle in the panes and the wood floor squeak beneath her feet. The good dishes in the hutch tinkled as she gained speed, bypassing the kitchen and the tea waiting to be made, running blind.

She couldn't get far enough away or fast enough. She grasped the smooth doorknob and pulled, flying down the steps two at a time in the dark. She couldn't escape the remembered words from their conversation that prickled her as if she were a pincushion, merciless and without end.

Are you telling me you remembered that from high school?

You'd be surprised what I noticed about you.

I thought I annoyed you.

How could anyone so lovely and smart be annoying? I always liked you.

So, he'd waited until after the wedding to tell her

that? She agreed to marry him because he didn't like her, as in the loving kind of like. She'd bound herself to this man who could bring endless destruction in her life—because that's what love did.

I don't think I can do this. She hit the concrete floor and there was nowhere left to run. The unfinished walls were still studs. The extra freezer was down here, humming quietly, and the furnace fan flicked on, driving the central air. The cavernous dark only echoed back to her the rugged, raw sound of her breathing, and it sounded strangely like sobs. Which was impossible because she wasn't crying. She was *not*.

Jared would only bring her misery, whether he meant to or not. He'd never intended to make this a friendship deal. No, he had an ulterior motive in all this. Falling in love wouldn't be the best thing for her, it wouldn't make the boys any happier.

What children needed was a good decent father who cared about them. Harmony. Knowing their parents could get along, solve problems and provide a safe environment for them. That's what mattered. It went without saying they both loved the boys, but beyond that, anything else was a recipe for disaster. Trusting someone only led to the inevitable breaking of that trust.

Hadn't Eddie proved that to her? In less than an hour, maybe two tops, Jared would be moving his things in. He'd be taking over her house, taking over her life and she had the rising fear that he had never intended to keep this equal. A team project.

He wanted her heart. He wanted everything. She had nothing more left to give. Eddie had taken everything, he'd taken it all, everything but her son. And left her with debt, doubt, emotional devastation and the hollow truth that she'd been a fool to ever trust him.

The phone jingled upstairs. It rang a few times. She couldn't make herself go up to answer it. Let it ring. It was probably her mother calling from an exotic and exciting destination, because she thought Luke's birthday was today instead of next month.

Jared's steps knelled overhead. "Meg? Is it all right if I get that? It's my mom."

Just answer it, she wanted to tell him, but he didn't know where she was and she wanted it to stay that way. He'd pitched his voice down the hallway, thinking she was in her bedroom.

Jared's conversation drifted down from the open door, easy and friendly. He was a man who would stay, who was committed, who would not walk away from Luke. It was the reason she could take a deep breath and resolve to put aside her fear, as much as she could. She didn't know if God could hear her. She didn't know if her prayers would matter. But she prayed away, wishing, simply wishing for the boys' happiness.

I can take what comes, she decided, *as long as they are happy. Because I love them.*

She heard Jared on the stairs, by the time she'd dragged out most of the empty boxes. His voice carried to her in the shadows.

"Meg? Mom said the boys are busy keeping her entertained. She said they slept through the night in the same room. This morning, they both ate two whole pancakes and some sausage. Oh, and I put Buster in the backyard. I hope you don't mind." His steps halted behind her. "Hey, let me get that."

He leaned close, and she stepped away before her

senses could register the woodsy, manly scent of him. The faint spice of his aftershave. The laundry softener fresh on his clothes. Before she could wish that—just once—fairy tales could come true.

She could feel his gaze on her as she retreated. Her spirit felt a tug as she took the first stair and then the next, rising out of the dark and into the brazen sunshine blazing through the miniblinds. The cats sat on the chair cushions, peering out through the rungs in the chair backs, where they had clear views of the lawn through the bay window. A brown streak zipped from sprinkler head to sprinkler head, enjoying the blast of the water.

"What do you think of your new brother?" she asked the cats, although it was fairly clear they did not approve at all of any creature who lacked dignity.

Buster was another silver lining to this marriage. She'd always wanted a dog. She wanted Luke to have a dog to grow up with, and she'd lacked the strength to take on the raising of a puppy after the divorce was final. This was a perfect solution.

She set the microwave and while it hummed, she filled a big bowl with cool water and opened the back French door.

The brown streak let out an excited yipping yowl, plowed straight through the middle of the water-drenched lawn and bounded up the steps. Meg barely had time to set down the bowl before the dog leaped up, put his paws on her shoulders and gave her a loving swipe of his tongue across her chin.

"Well, hello, I like you, too." Plus, she could always use the comic relief.

The door jerked open and there was Jared, stern-faced. "Down! What are you doing? I said, down!"

The Lab looked contrite and dropped to his haunches. His ears went down. His nose bowed to the ground in utter dejection.

Jared turned to her, surveying her from her sandals to her khaki shorts to her cotton blouse. "Meg, he got you all—"

Buster chose that moment to shake vigorously, spraying water droplets all over them.

"Wet." Jared finished and swiped the wetness from his face and eyes.

Meg's heart melted. As she knelt to comfort the dog. "You know what they say, like puppy, like master."

Jared knelt down, too close, too near, too everything. A tiny grin hooked the corner of his mouth. "You've said that."

"I hadn't realized how true it was until I met Buster."

"He's a great guy. Loyal. A good friend. He and I have that in common." Did she hear what he was really saying, Jared wondered.

Maybe, he judged, by the way she was quietly studying him. Water droplets splashed across the front of her shirt and dotted her face, clinging like tiny jewels in her rich, lustrous auburn hair. Like the wind, he dared to touch her. His fingertips feathered through her luxurious red locks. "Are you going to be all right sharing your house with a guy like me?"

"It's going to be tough, but I think I can survive it. Just keep plying me with doughnuts."

"I noticed you have a lot of room in your basement. Maybe when I come back from my next assignment, I can have Ben Cavanaugh come over and we'll put up wallboard. Would that be a help to you?"

"A help to me? I guess it would give us more room.

My house is small, and there are going to be four of us in this house. Eight, counting Buster and the cats."

Buster's tail thumped in a happy, crazy rhythm and then he couldn't take it anymore. He leaped up to bark and jump at the hummingbirds who dared to stay out of his reach.

Jared had to rewind his thoughts and concentrate on what Meg said. Or rather, what she hadn't said. He tried again. "If I'm out of line, you say. It's still your house, but if you want, I'd be happy to hire Ben to finish your downstairs."

"It's your house now, Jared."

"Our house." His soul wrenched and he could feel the pain inside her as surely as if one of the sprinkler heads had gone wonky, changed direction and hit him square in the face. But he wouldn't know it to look at her.

Her chin hitched, and the gentle breezes stirred her hair as she managed a small smile, barely one at all. Her quiet blue eyes were dark, but that was the only physical hint that this was hurting her. And he knew it wasn't about the house, it wasn't about moving his things in and disturbing hers. It wasn't about her having her way or anything.

"Okay, beautiful lady. Let's get this straight. You want a friendship. You want to work as a team. That's a marriage."

She looked at the flowerpots, the patio, the hummingbird feeder, at everything but him. "You want a *marriage.*"

"Yeah. Friendship, teamwork, caring for one another. It's pretty much the same."

She scrubbed the dog's chin, making him moan and

his back leg thump against the concrete. "Maybe for men."

"You do know I'm nothing like Eddie, right?"

"You're deeply religious, you have a hugely competitive job and you lead a Bible Study group. Hmm. Sounds the same." But she winked. "There are a lot of differences. I'm trusting my son's heart to you. That ought to say everything."

"It does, but I want to know what's hurting you, so I can make sure I don't do one thing that ever makes you think that I intend to hurt you."

Kindness. It wasn't something Meg expected from a man. But from Jared…she was afraid to get used to it. To believe in it. She wished she could lay her cheek against the strong plane of his chest and hold him tight. Just hold on. To believe that she wasn't alone, adrift at sea. That even if she were feeling overwhelmed, if her heart was broken beyond repair, that Jared was an unyielding anchor.

How did she trust that he would be there in the future? Was there anyone anywhere who had a marriage like that? She'd never seen one. Not her parents; a more cold distant relationship could not exist anywhere. Her grandparents? They'd passed on now, but she remembered their marriage had been similar.

"My experience of marriage wasn't the best. There's a reason why they say studies show that married men are the most happy, and married women are the most unhappy groups of people." She hated how rough her voice sounded and raw with pain she did not want Jared to know about. But Buster whined and licked her chin and cheek and nose.

"Stop," Jared ordered, reaching to pull his dog away.

Buster was her dog now, too, and she wound her arms around his sturdy neck and hugged back, breathing in the wet doggy scent of him and loving the sleek sensation of his fur.

"Tell me," Jared said. "What was so bad?"

How could she tell him how the misery had become so gradual? She'd worked so hard trying to make her marriage work. She'd given up little pieces of herself until she was hollow. She'd compromised and bent and bowed until she'd snapped into pieces she'd put back together again. But she wasn't the same.

The doorbell pealed, reverberating through the house and out the door, which was cracked open just a bit. Buster barked, taking off like a wild thing to the door, which he nudged open with his nose. His doggy feet flailed and pounded on the polished hardwood floor, his delighted barks drowning out the sound of the chime.

"That would be Chris and Ramon. I'll invite them in, offer them doughnuts and tea. Did you still want to come along? You can pick through my townhouse and decide what you want to bring here and what goes to the neighboring church thrift store."

She didn't trust herself to speak. Jared, friendly and confident and unshakable, strode away, the tone of his voice amused by his dog's antics. She waited until she heard the door open and men's voices before she grabbed the hose and tended to the hand watering.

The mist from the sprinklers felt luxurious on her face. She missed her little boy, she missed being in control of her own life, she missed the young woman she'd used to be, that high school girl full of innocence and romance. Her spirit ached with a dull throbbing pain, like arthritis in an old wound. Where was God? She'd stopped believing that He was in charge of her life, working to make good things for her future.

Then, as if in answer, the sunshine danced through the tall trees shadowing the yard to gleam on the swing set sitting idle and still, glistening with the dampness from the sprinklers. Maybe it was an answer. Maybe it was simply the result of the rotation of the earth around the sun, but for whatever reason it gave her enough strength to face the day as a wife.

As the sun set on a good day of productive work, Jared couldn't get his friend's words out of his head. He and Chris had been hefting the couch down the steps to Meg's basement and they'd stopped for a breather. Puffing and panting, they'd taken a few moments and Chris said, "You've got yourself a fine wife. It's a shame what Talbot put her through. Meg is a nice lady."

What *did* Eddie put her through? Jared had been about to ask, but Ramon and Meg had come in to the house and so he held off. He hadn't gotten a chance to corner Chris and ask him what he knew.

He'd offered to treat his friends to dinner, but they declined, and said they'd be looking forward to seeing him at Bible Study. Jared found Meg in the kitchen, reorganizing her cupboards to accommodate the kitchen appliances of his that she didn't have. He was surprised by what she'd said he could pack. Everything from a toaster oven to a hand mixer to the electric skillet.

He stood in the archway, watching her in the kitchen, and from his vantage he could see the top shelves of the cupboards. The cabinet doors were open and Meg rearranged and readjusted, and he was surprised how little was actually in her cupboards. Only the bare essentials.

A stack of mixing bowls. Practical dishes that, he realized, looked practically brand-new. Almost everything did.

He saw it now. The kitchen table was very nice-looking, but it was new and it wasn't expensive. The furniture, the few pictures on the wall.

"How's it coming?" he asked, and she startled, as if she'd been lost in thought and hadn't heard him.

"I thought I would put the things we might use more in the lower cabinets. I put your skillet here." She moved over toward the stove and opened a bottom cabinet door. "And this air popcorn popper might get a lot of use, so I put it down here, too, where it's easier to reach."

"You like popcorn, do you?"

"A weakness, I know. Is this all right?"

Funny, but that was never a question Vanessa had asked him. She did what she wanted with the kitchen, but Meg was watching him with measuring eyes, as if she were trying to peer deep into his soul. Or gauge his reaction. Eddie had been controlling, had he?

"Whatever you want," he told her. "I want you to feel comfortable in your own kitchen, which reminds me. Food. Do you want to swing by Mom's, grab the boys and pick up burgers at the drive-thru?"

"The one on West or the one on Main?"

"West. The ones with the killer onion rings. Remember how we all used to hang out there in high school?"

"Another thing you noticed from back then?"

"I'm a reporter. I notice everything. Well, I try." He held out his hand. "Let's go pick up our boys."

Slow and steady, he vowed, showing her the way it was going to be married to him. He opened the door for her and held the screen door while she locked up. He helped her into the SUV and closed her door. He ignored the fact that she watched him with questioning eyes the entire four-block drive to his mom's house.

The boys were standing on the couch, hands and faces pressed against the glass. By the time Jared climbed out, leaving the air-conditioning running, the door was open and two identical toddlers were laughing as they bounded down the brick walkway.

"Mama!" Luke shouted, holding up his half-eaten sugar cookie.

Chance squealed and ran right to Meg, too, holding up his cookie to show her.

"Did Gramma make these? Are they yummy?"

"Yum!" Luke emphasized with great glee.

"Mmmm." Chance did his best to communicate.

Wow, the little guy must really be needing a mom. Jared wasn't used to having his son run to someone else like that, but he didn't mind. How could anyone not adore Meg? She'd knelt so she was eye level, speaking gently and lovingly to the twins. Gently smoothing Luke's hair into place and rubbing a crumb from Chance's rosy cheek.

He'd never missed Vanessa more than at this moment, when he realized she'd been replaced. No, that wasn't exactly right—he'd never missed her like this, in a way that felt as if she were truly gone from his life forever.

Chance had a family. He had a mother to love him again. Jared had a new wife, a partner for this life. As if the breeze were a hand lifting upward, it lingered for one brief, soft moment. Then it was gone. Forever gone.

Maybe it was just his writer's nature, he thought,

reading messages into a simple evening breeze. But that didn't explain the wave of loneliness crashing through him, drowning his heart and his spirit until he could feel nothing else.

Nothing at all.

Until Meg, hugging the boys close, smiled up at him over the top of their matching downy heads, and he realized he was no longer alone.

Chapter Twelve

"Ham-burg! Ham-burg!" Luke chanted, smacking his highchair tray.

Chance joined in, even before Meg had him locked in safe and sound. His sweet eyes gazed shyly up at her. "Hmmm!" He lurched sideways, restrained by his buckle, toward the white paper sack overfilled with crisp, golden fries.

"Careful, little one." She smoothed her hand down his back, distracting him. He grinned up at her, blue eyes wide, brimming with innocence.

"Fwies!" Luke demanded with a fist to his tray and both boys laughed at the sound of the tray rattling.

Both sets of fists began to pound, and the noise along with the boy's happy sounds filled the cozy kitchen and nook area with a rare joy. Meg's soul filled; it was like a door being opened and sunlight rushing in. Except it was a powerful, raw-edged love crashing through her, illuminating every shadow and spilling through every crack until she felt new.

Meg couldn't stop the tide of love crashing through her.

"All right, all right." Jared looked as happy as she felt as he hooked the tub of French fries from the sack and dumped a decent amount on each boys' tray. Their giggles turned into contented chewing as those small fists filled with the golden treats.

Buster sat statue-straight a few feet behind the high chairs, a safe distance away from the table. His bright eyes and wagging tail swept the floor in fast arcs, on guard for the first fry to hit the deck. Meg couldn't help it—she tossed him a French fry and he caught it neatly, keeping his haunches on the floor, as polite as could be.

The cats scattered, deciding to watch the circus from a quieter location.

"Here's your tartar." She popped the top from the plastic cup and set the first one on Chance's tray, who looked up at her, clutching a half-eaten fry in his sticky hand.

"Watch," she told him as she opened a second container and before she had it flat on Luke's tray, he was dunking his fries into it.

He took a big bite and grinned. "Yummm."

Chance mimicked him and they howled as if they'd done the funniest thing in the entire world.

"That's good for a person's heart, isn't it?" Jared looked transformed. The tension had erased completely off his face. The tiny furrows in his forehead and deeper lines bracketing his mouth had vanished. He seemed to stand a little straighter, although that could have been her imagination.

"It's certainly good for my heart." She couldn't look at him as she unwrapped the first hamburger, and Luke was already grabbing for it. She unwrapped the second and Chance, repeating his brother's move, reached up and snatched it from her with both hands.

"Yummm." Luke beamed, with ketchup smearing his lip.

"Hmmmm," Chance seconded, with mustard on his chin.

Jared poured two unspillable cups with milk and set one on each tray. The healthful drink was ignored as the twins ate burgers like hungry baby birds.

"This one's yours." Jared placed a cheeseburger on a plate and held it toward the table. "Which chair do you want?"

"I'll sit on this side of the boys."

"Practical. Then I guess I'll sit over here."

One on each side. Just the way Meg needs it to be, Jared thought, as he pulled out the wooden chair and settled into it. Chris's words stuck with him.

What Jared didn't get was how any man could be unkind to a woman as nice as Meg? She had worked hard all day, although she'd been courteous and a lot more withdrawn than he'd liked. But he was beginning to figure out how badly she must have been hurt, and not just from the aftermath of Eddie's discovered affairs.

She shone when she was with the boys. She unwrapped her cheeseburger without even noticing what she was doing. All her attention was focused on the little ones. Their joy was her joy.

"I almost forgot grace." He couldn't believe it. He had his super burger unwrapped and was ready to take a huge bite. "I'm starved, so here it is."

"Not, 'Good God, Good Food, Amen'?"

"Amen. I couldn't have said it better." Jared felt his chest hitch—his heart skipped a beat and the silence pulsed in his ears.

The inner silence of a pivotal, life-changing mo-

ment. Meg was doing this to him without even knowing it, with the quiet gentleness that shone through her
like dawn through clouds—and his entire being ached
with the power of it. With the longing to make her shine
like this all the time. And more.

She was not the same Meg he remembered from
high school, he realized, taking a bite of his burger
while he watched her daintily tug the pickle slices from
between the beef patty and bun and toss each one,
drenched with ketchup and mustard, into the nearest
empty food sack.

While that was something the teenaged Meg would
have done, he saw the ghostly image of the past super-
impose over his sight. Younger, bubblier, her face soft,
with no life experiences or character yet imprinted on
her lovely features, laughing easily with her friends.

Sitting at the Starlight Diner, which had been not too
far from the high school, after classes, her lustrous red
hair perfectly coifed and curled. She was radiant, like
a magazine model with everything right, everything
matching, and yet a sweet girl-next-door brightness to
her as she pulled pickles from her cheeseburger.

He was a journalist. He noticed details, and yet the
past slipped away and with it the adoring type of first
love he'd felt for her. They'd both changed. He was no
longer the poor kid sitting on the sidelines, away from
the popular kids, with an old camera his mom had
picked up at a garage sale. He'd fought hard, earned his
way and liked to think he had more substance these
days. And his love for Meg had more substance, too.

Because that's what this keenly painful twist in his
soul was—love, deep and true. And it was a one-way
street, at least that part of things hadn't changed. But it

had become something different. Something that left him unable to think, breathe normally, or reach to keep Chance from shoving all his fries off the tray. Meg had to do it in her competent, easy and gentle way. Buster let out a moan of disappointment and thumped his tail on the floor. Meg stole a fry from her sack and slipped him one.

"Uhhh!" Chance protested, opening his mouth wide.

Without hesitation, Meg snared a fry, plunked it into the tartar and slipped it into his mouth.

Jared's soul sighed.

"Da-dee! Da-dee!" Luke demanded with brilliant enthusiasm, looking up at Jared with an innocent plea. "Please!"

"Pee-z," Chance begged despite his handful of fries remaining.

He doled out more fries, too full to speak. Emotions rose within him like a hot spring, bubbling up from his innermost being. Gratitude. Commitment. Love.

For where your treasure is, there will your heart be also—the passage came to him like a touch on his shoulder.

His heart was here and all he treasured. After nearly two years of feeling adrift, he'd found his anchor.

He was home.

"I don't know about you, but I'm beat."

As Meg stretched out her aching muscles that had tightened up while she'd sat still at the table, her new wedding ring glinted and sparkled. It was strange, having a ring there once again when she'd gotten used to a bare finger.

At first that had been a strange sensation and a painful reminder that her marriage had ended. Badly, inevitably. The space on her left ring finger was, for several months, a reminder of her inadequacies.

A reminder of how easily she'd been fooled, how easily she'd trusted when she'd known good and well something was wrong in her marriage, and how desperately she'd wanted Eddie's love—and he hadn't wanted her.

Not her. No, he'd desired another. When she'd worked, typing at the computer, she couldn't stop being aware that her two-carat diamond wasn't turning on her finger. But in time, she began to realize the upside of being on her own again.

Now, Jared's beautiful ring, sporting its four inset diamonds, felt like shackles.

"Down! Down! Down!" Luke squealed, hands and face sticky with ketchup and mustard and tartar and bits of hamburger.

Chance imitated with a yell.

"All right." Meg grabbed a napkin, dunked it in her water glass and began to rub the stickiness off her son's fists. And then her other son's. Both boys resisted with appropriate "ah, mom" sorts of grimaces.

The instant Luke's tennis shoes hit the floor, he pounded across the room, hopped onto the brick hearth and stretched up on tiptoe.

The overhead lights plunged into darkness. The ceiling fan stopped rotating and slowed, the fins swishing to a stop.

Chance laughed in glee and clapped his hands.

"Hey, there, big boy, leave the light on." After the light snapped back on, she lowered Chance to the ground and he took off, clapping his hands. "Is it time for your bath?"

"No!" Luke squealed.

"Oh!" Chance danced up and down, wanting Luke to turn the light off.

Behind her, Jared began clearing the table. "I usually do the dishes after I get Luke to bed." She couldn't quite believe that Jared was crumpling up discarded wrappers and empty tartar containers. "I'll clean up the kitchen after I get these two tucked in."

Jared shrugged. "Need help corralling them?"

"It's my job."

Luke ran shrieking, "No! No! No!" Laughing with his comrade, who tailed him shouting in an identical, joy-filled voice. "No! No! No!" They made a lap around the living room and Jared touched her shoulder.

It was a light touch, but as sustaining as moonlight. He leaned close so that his breath was a warm shiver against her ear. "We're partners, remember? I'll go fill the tub."

Had she heard him right? She did a double take and, sure enough, Jared was heading down the hallway, whistling.

Whistling.

It was fine that he was in a good mood, but would it last? She wasn't going to count on it. This was their first night of being a family together. She intended to take this marriage moment by moment.

But as she heard the water crashing into the bathtub, she dared to hope. A little. Deciding to bring the boys together in one household was a sound one. Look at how happy they looked, running and giggling and shouting "No!"

Buster had situated himself in the archway, as if he felt it was his duty to watch over the little ones. She rested her hand on the top of his warm velvet head and he smiled up at her. He was a great companion for the boys.

"Hey, you two! Bath time. Let's go!" She clapped her hands and Luke skidded to a stop and Chance bumped into him.

The boys laughed and laughed.

Happiness echoed in the room like music and lifted her heart. Filled her right up. She took hold of two identical shoulders, gently steering them toward the archway. Buster gave Luke a big sloppy kiss on the side of his face.

As he stopped to laugh and wiped at his cheek, the dog got the other boy. Chance laughed and took off down the hallway, leading Luke. Meg caught up with them just in time to watch Jared barrel down the hall, growling like a bear. Chance howled and shrieked as Jared grabbed his son around the waist and turned him upside down.

"I got ya now!" He anchored his son against his hip.

Luke was laughing, stomping his feet. "Up! Up!"

And Jared complied, whipping him upside down and swinging both boys until they howled and screamed with joy.

"I'm going to dunk you both. Headfirst!"

He disappeared through the bathroom doorway with both giggling boys, the light tossing his shadow into the doorway. Meg watched as Jared's shadow shortened, as he knelt to the ground and gently turned each boy onto his feet. His low voice came loving and kind.

Emotions too difficult to name, too powerful to measure rose like cream to the top as she leaned against the doorjamb and watched both little boys radiate with happiness.

"We'll get it all set up for Mom," he was telling them. "Towels. Shampoo. Tub boys."

"Frow!" Luke clasped his little hands together, overwhelmed with excitement.

"Oh!" Chance agreed.

"Frow? Oh, I get it. You mean throw. Okay, where does she keep the toys?" He looked around at the tidy bathroom. "Your mom is the kind to have lots of tub toys. Maybe in the cabinet?"

"The other side." She knelt to assist him, their shoulders brushing as she tugged open the cabinet door. Before she could lift the bright yellow beach pail brimming with toys, Jared had reached in front of her to do it.

She felt an awareness of emotion deep within her spirit. Jared's biceps rippled beneath the bronzed skin and the hem of his short-sleeved shirt. He seemed substantial, as if he could handle any problem. A good man to trust.

Tempting. Meg swallowed hard and took the toys from him. Luke was in the process of stepping out of his cute little denim shorts and yanking at the tags of his diapers.

"Frow!" He ran naked to the edge of the tub, reaching up for the bright bucket.

Chance, in the process of nearly hanging himself with his shirt removal, stopped to bang his one freed fist against the edge of the tub.

"Here, little guy." She lowered the toys into the center of the garden tub with one hand, while Luke grunted trying to reach them, and freed Chance from his shirt with her other hand.

"Yours has a talent for undressing, does he?" Jared hooked Luke under the arms and lowered him into the tub.

Above the splashing, Meg unsnapped Chance's shorts and tugged off his sneakers. Chance, sweet as cherry pie, filled his fist with her shirtsleeve while he lifted his right foot. Affection tugged deep within her for this little boy who was just like Luke, and yet wasn't.

She hooked off his shoe and removed the other. Jared reached over, divested him of his diaper and plopped him into the water across from Luke.

"Frow!" Luke was demonstrating his acumen with the plastic primary colored rings.

Other toys floated up out of the bucket—floating fish, boats, seaplanes, balls, ducks and whales.

"Need any help?"

Meg was reaching for the shampoo bottle and had to look back over her shoulder at him. He stood in the doorway, the light burnishing the rugged lines on his face. He looked adventurous, like the award-winning journalist he was. He also looked completely sincere. And just how domestic was a world-traveling man?

"I've got it. Go downstairs and check out the satellite dish. I have tons of news channels. I know you mentioned wanting to play with the remote."

"Guilty. You know I would." He saluted her like a soldier—a very disarmingly dangerous one.

That couldn't be a good thing, that her soul stirred. He left, and a wave of very warm water slapped across her front. The splashing glee of the boys making tidal waves at each other needed to be put to a stop. She did so gently, and then started on Luke's hair.

He good-naturedly put up with the scrubbing as long as he could throw everything that drifted toward him into the water. The kerplunks enthralled Chance, who splashed with approval.

It was hard not to like being a mom of twins. She started to sing one of Luke's favorite songs as she scrubbed Chance's hair, a Sunday school rhyme she'd learned long ago. Chance hummed, too, although he didn't know the song or was anywhere near the key, while Luke kept a sort of percussion as he dropped the toys in the water.

When she reached for the hand attachment and turned it on, she felt the change of pressure as she adjusted the temperature. Was Jared using water? The faint clink of dishes confirmed it. She was dying to see if he was just making a pot of tea or something, or if he was washing the lunch and supper dishes.

He couldn't be. She refused to believe it as she rained down warm clear water over two soapy heads, and the sound of their squeals drowned out the kitchen sounds.

Jared squirted dishwashing soap into the little cup, clicked the cover shut and started the dishwasher. Over the whir and groaning of the machine, he could still hear the happy sounds of the boys. *She's great with them.*

She'd let the tub water out over ten minutes ago— he was keeping his eye on the clock—and the sounds now came from the back bedroom. The nightly struggle to get into pajamas and brush their teeth was in full swing, he figured, and wondered if she needed a hand.

"Jesus loves the little children, all the children of the world…." Her clear soprano lifted faintly through the house.

He rinsed the dishcloth and wiped down the counter, working quickly, wanting to hurry up and join his family. But in his heart he wanted Meg to have her time with them, too.

Then suddenly, there they were, shouting and racing down the hall, clean, baby-shampoo scented and dressed in soft knit pajamas—their matching ones. Bare feet slapped on the hard wood and Luke and Chance ran neck and neck through the eating nook and into his arms.

Shouts of "Da-dee" and "Dada!" echoed in the high ceilings above.

How did a man describe how his heart filled with love for his sons? Or for his wife, who'd fostered such happiness in them?

He only knew he was on his knees and two wiggling little boys filled his arms. Bright eyes and rosy faces and their fragile warmth snuggling against him. He kissed both matching foreheads, letting their joy filter into him. "Bedtime."

"No-oo!" Luke gave his best charming grin, perhaps hoping to get a little more playtime out of the deal.

Jared stood firm. He was used to a little boy's charm. Chance was looking around a little confused, as if he wasn't quite sure where to go. He knew where his crib was in his grandma's house and in his house, but he hadn't figured out yet that he was here for good.

"Let's go check out your new digs, sport." He captured two hands in his. "Let's march! Hut, one, two, three, four!"

The boys eagerly joined in the marching and the shouting. The pound of feet and the echo of their voices filled the house with happiness as he let the twins haul him past an irresistible Meg and down the hallway to the light spilling out of the door at the end of the way.

The boys' room was pretty fine. Meg had decorated it as a boy's nursery, and there were still those baby touches everywhere. The walls above the wainscoting had been painted a restful baby blue and a roll of that wallpaper border stuff topped it off. Colorful trains and teddy bears and balloons ribboned around the room.

Meg had made up Chance's crib with care and placed it across the room from Luke's where the boys could face one another while they slept. A rocking chair—one she'd probably rocked Luke to sleep in for innumerable nights when he'd been a baby—sat between them beneath the closed drapes of the generous window. A toy box was wedged into the corner, too full for the lid to close all the way. And a series of bigger toys, a chunky plastic car garage and a train yard waited quietly in the dark corner.

A fine room for little boys to laugh and play and grow in. He swept each toddler off the ground and deposited them in their appropriate cribs.

Chance sank to his knees and stuck his thumb in his mouth, gazing around, taking in his new place. A half dozen boxes sat stacked in the corner. Chance's toys and clothes still needed to be unpacked, but that could wait until tomorrow. For tonight, he had all he would need.

Luke had collapsed onto his stomach, with his knees tucked beneath him so his diapered bottom stuck out and the blanket and sheet were pulled over his head.

"The right way, there, Mr. Luke." He folded the edge of the covers.

Luke appeared, grinning wide. "Boo!"

Jared acted surprised, making the little guy giggle. Chance joined in without knowing why.

Her gaze breezed against him and he turned to her, feeling her presence move through his spirit. This strange awareness of her could frighten him, for he'd never felt anything like it before, not with Vanessa, not with anyone. It was as if his soul acknowledged hers, and when he saw her watching him with wide, quiet eyes from the shadowed hallway, he knew without question she felt less doubt. Less fear. From simply watching him parent her son. Sons, now.

And I'll be just as good to you. The thought came with such power, he felt it rip through his soul, and she seemed to startle, as if she'd heard it without him needing to say the words.

Or maybe he'd imagined it as she bowed her head, so the shadows hid her features from him and he could not read her emotions, but he still felt all of her hurt.

How, Jared wondered, could any man not see the precious treasure of this woman? Of her open heart that loved children, of her soft nature that made sure hummingbirds were fed and spent her first moments of the day watching the sun rise and watering her flowers?

She'd come to believe she had nothing to fear from him. Certain of his purpose, he and the boys said a prayer and he kissed them both good-night. Meg moved past him, to kiss each warm forehead and smooth back tangled, fine blond hair, and switched on the small child's lamp on the chest of drawers, tucked on the short wall next to the door.

Heart in his throat, Jared watched as she flipped off the overhead light.

"Sleep well, my darlings."

She moved past him like music, soft and sweet and poignant, through the shadows to the main bathroom. Jared stood in the hall, unable to move, listening to the sounds as she gathered the wet towels and clothes and dumped them into the hamper.

Inside their room, the twins were making noises at one another and giggling. He closed the door. They'd had a long day, and their tummies were full. They'd drift off soon enough, but what did he do about Meg? It was nearly nine o'clock and she was still working.

"Thanks for your help, Jared." Her back was to him as she swabbed up the water on the floor with the last of the towels the twins had gone through. "I can't believe how Luke has taken to you. You've been more of a father to him already than Eddie ever was. That means a lot to him. And to me."

"Me, too." He twisted the towel from her grip and tossed it into the hamper. "Two points."

"Basketball. I remember cheering you on."

"You were the best cheerleader."

"Oh, it seems so long ago. There's no spring to my step tonight, that's for sure. We got a lot done today, don't you think?" Without waiting for him to answer and purposefully ignoring his overture of simple human connection, she headed out of the bathroom and down the hall, mentally clicking off the chores still needing to be done.

There was safety in distance, she'd learned the hard way. Distance was the inevitable situation between a man and wife. She wasn't about to start getting her hopes up, only to be defeated. Although, with the loving way he'd treated Luke, as equally strong and loving as with Chance, it made it desperately difficult to keep her defenses up, her battered heart protected and her self-control in place.

She flicked on the light to the kitchen and the sudden brightness spotlighted pristine countertops and every dish washed and put away. Except for one thing. A cup of tea steeping on the breakfast bar and a pot of honey beside it.

"Thought you might like some chamomile tea and

honey to wind down with," he explained, as if he'd done nothing extraordinary. As if he hadn't taken a dynamite charge to her defensive shields and obliterated them. "I'm gonna catch the TV news back in my room. Is there anything more I can do for you?"

She shook her head, unable to speak, emotion unraveling in her heart. She couldn't move until she heard the click of his bedroom door and the barely discernible murmur of the television.

Her hands shook. All of her started to shake. She sat down in the nearest chair before she fell down, feeling the tears she'd never shed after that initial horrible night over discovering Eddie's final affair. Scalding, soul-breaking tears that rolled silently up and out of her. She finally had the husband she'd always prayed for, but she couldn't love him. She could never love any man, not ever again.

Lost in her sorrow, she didn't notice the small rasp of a door opening. Or the shadow in the hallway standing alone, hands fisted, full of sorrow, too.

Chapter Thirteen

"I didn't mean to make you cry." Jared's voice seemed to come out of nowhere.

"You aren't." She swiped at her face, but there was too much wetness, too many tears. Suddenly he was there, kneeling beside her, a strong tender man she had no right needing. She shouldn't be letting so much of her vulnerable side show. She was raw, unguarded, without shields or defenses and he could hurt her right now, with her heart exposed. "I didn't thank you for all that you did today. You are a considerate man—"

"Don't pretend nothing's wrong."

"Nothing is. Not really." She mustered up what inner strength she could find, not that she could find much in the tattered mess she'd become. She'd pretend nothing was wrong, because that way, maybe she could will it to be true. It had to be true, because she wasn't going to make a mistake this time. Not when her sons' happiness was on the line.

She took a steadying breath and automatically a prayer seemed to fill her head, she'd never gotten out of the habit of it. In truth, she'd never wanted to. Just because she didn't hear God didn't mean that God couldn't hear her.

Please, help me to be strong. Help me to keep my feet on the ground. I don't want to ruin it this time around. She wouldn't go wishing for something that could never exist.

Because she couldn't look into his caring eyes for another single second, she took another ragged breath and swiped the last of her tears with her napkin, tossed it on the counter and stood as if she'd never been crying at all.

She wove around him and headed to the glass door. "I've still got the hand watering to do—"

"Meg, forget the watering."

"The flowers wouldn't be too happy with that." She managed a weak grin, as if she wasn't at all close to crying again. As if the vision of Jared kneeling before her empty chair didn't make her want to believe that fairy-tale wishes could come true.

He was unbelievable, a big strong capable guy perfect in just about every way, at least on the surface, with the tea he'd brewed and took the time to set out honey.

Panic roared through her like thunder, and she couldn't stop it from taking over. She sailed out the door and into the humid night where she was finally, utterly and forever alone.

Luke needs him, I can see that, Lord, but I don't. I won't.

The doorknob behind her turned and the hinges whispered open. She could feel Jared moving toward her. It was as if her spirit was a flower turning to face the sun and she could not move away from him. The connection to him felt so strong, it didn't change or diminish when she turned her back to him and started walking fast and hard. Distance and willpower had no sway on the binds that tied them soul to soul. A bond she did not want to admit existed. She did not want to believe in.

Please, Lord, she prayed with all her might, *release me from this bond. It only makes my heart hurt more.*

And it was. Like ice cracking apart, shattering in a billion infinitesimal shards, she swore she could hear the snap, and pain left her gasping for breath as she felt her heart break more widely apart. And her entire being felt wide open and exposed, like a deep wound with the bandage suddenly ripped off and stung by the fresh air. She felt as if it was her that was crackling apart, piece by piece, and she grabbed the hose, twisted the faucet on and kept going. *I am not going to let you know what you do to me, Jared Kierney.*

"Meg?"

She squeezed the nozzle handle and a gentle rain showered from the wide end over the colorful flowers, looking a little wilted form the day's heat. *Just keep thinking about the flowers and not about—*

Jared. His soothing hands curved around her shoulders, and out of the far corner of her eye she saw the faint glimmer of his wedding band. Mocking her? Or reminding her? Was it a sign from above? Or a trick of the light?

"I don't know what I've done, sweet lady, but I sure wish you would tell me what's hurting you."

Her frozen heart crackled even more. Did he have to sound so kind? Did he have to make her feel as if he would take care of her, protect her and defend her, that his warm presence enveloped her like the most tender of hugs and she couldn't feel anything except fear. Fear and the pain from what the last man who had also been handsome and funny when he wanted to be, had done to her heart, her spirit, her faith…her everything. When a man loved you, he knew just where to hit where it would hurt the most. What to say, what to criticize. What to do. What to promise.

"Meg, I just want to make things right between us."

"I'm only tired."

"You're tight." His thumbs dug into her vertebrae.

"Oh." Relief ripped through her coiled muscles. Her hand relaxed, and the nozzle silenced. She closed her eyes, not willing to move away. Yet. The stressed connective tissue and muscle fibers in her neck relaxed. Tears built in her eyes. His massage was firm, just short of painful, and yet she hadn't realized how sore and tight her neck was. Or how good it felt when Jared's hands moved away. She tilted her head to the side, stretching the newly unclenched muscles and it felt much better.

Then the heat of his lips pressed against the slight bump of her vertebrae. Affection radiated from him and seemed to fill up the cracks in her broken heart. She felt the heat of it searing hot against her frozen places within. It was too much feeling, too much pain, too much hope and she couldn't bear it. She broke away and the hose tumbled out of her hand. She stumbled forward, her shoe caught on the hose and down she went.

Time flashed into slow motion as gravity yanked her forward, her hands came up to stop her fall and the concrete patio rose up and slammed into her. The impact jerked from her palms to her knees. A different kind of pain—keen, physical pain razored from flesh to bone and then Jared was there at her side, on his knees, his touch comforting.

"Are you all right? Meg, you're bleeding."

"I'm klutzy." Embarrassed, she tried to twist around so she could get her feet underneath her and be on her way, but Jared gripped her around the waist, helping her up, helping her to stand. And she didn't want him, couldn't he see that? But she lacked the strength to push him away as his arm slipped around her shoulders and he led her over to the patio set and pulled out a chair for her.

"I was trying to tell you," he knelt before her and studied her scraped knees. "I already watered for you."

"The flowers?"

"Yep. Notice the drip marks?"

Sure enough, there were dark pools on the cement beneath the colorful pots and baskets and planters. "When did you do that?"

"I'm quick and I'm sneaky. When you're not looking, I'll sneak in a chore without telling you."

"This is just a newlywed thing, isn't it? You're trying to impress me now. I know you, Jared Kierney."

"You do. But you aren't acting like it. And you're not trusting what you know."

"About you?" She wanted to tell him that over a decade separated them from their high school years, and they'd both grown into different people.

But the look on his face stopped her. Her cynicism felt ugly, like smog clouding her soul. She couldn't see out. She couldn't see in. Trapped, she wondered, was there no way out?

Jared's touch seemed to grow stronger on her knee, although she could tell he wasn't pushing against her with any more force. It wasn't only comfort she felt. But like everything she'd dreamed of long ago when she'd believed in love and dreams and God, it all waited patiently as if at the end of a tunnel, but she was lost in the darkness and smog. Jared moved away, breaking his touch, breaking contact, and the connection died.

She felt the recoil within her like a rubber band breaking and snapping back with a sting. As if struck, she would have retreated, but there was nowhere to go. Jared kneeled before her, his big strong body blocking her way, and the wrought-iron chair she sat in had a high-cushioned back.

She would have to climb over the wide metal arms if she wanted out, and she couldn't summon up enough energy, even with panic whispering in her ear to move. To go. The boys were tucked in, the household chores done. There was no reason to even speak with Jared until morning, when the twins were awake.

Couldn't Jared see that he was destroying her? His kindness and his acts of caring and tender gestures and physical human touch reminded her she wasn't alone. She wasn't dead to the world. She still had a heart, somewhere, somehow, buried deep beneath the icy heart that still beat, that still felt.

Still dreamed.

With all that Eddie had put her through, pushing and pulling at her emotions, asking for endless forgiveness when he knew good and well that he was in the act of betraying her, and she was wrung out, like a cloth twisted of every ounce of water, and she was used up, no good for what Jared needed. For this marriage that he kept wanting to have with her.

The tiny part of her spirit that struggled to feel was nothing but pain, nothing but a weakness, and she laid a hand over her heart because it was the only protection she had. Feelings are what got a person in trouble. They'd certainty laid her in ruin. She had to be strong. She had to get control of her feelings and make them stop. But how? Jared was doing this to her. Jared, made more powerful by his tenderness as he took a handkerchief from his pocket and dabbed at her knees.

"It's not too bad. I think some antibiotic cream and a cartoon bandage—I think I have some in one of Chance's boxes."

Did Jared know what affect his dimpled smile had on her? It was infectious and she had to fight from responding. She squeezed her eyes shut and stared past his wide shoulders to the back fence. A robin perched there, surveying the lush grass, and spread its wings. She watched the creature soar upward to land in an old magnolia tree. She longed, too, to escape.

"You have to learn to trust God, Meg." He didn't come across pedantic. She could see nothing but sincerity in him. She could feel the deep unbending certainty of his faith.

"I tried that." She closed her heart against the pain and disappointment. "I did trust Him. Over and over again. When I didn't have anything more left in me, I still forgave Eddie. I honored the promises I made. I did everything I could and I'm just empty. I'm just wrung out. I was the one who forgave. I was the one who had faith. All it did was break me. It made me a fool."

"You're not a fool. Not you, Meg."

"You don't understand. How can you? You don't know. No one does."

Jared could feel the wound inside her, dark as a total eclipse. Like night when it should have been full daylight. He cupped her jaw, holding her face in his hands, and the instant his skin contacted hers, he felt the bleak dark hopelessness inside her. His throat swelled so that it was hard to breathe. Or maybe that was the feeling of pain rising in his chest, hers as if it were his. And he marveled at that. At the way things worked out in a man's life.

That when he'd thought he'd lost the most important love of his life, Meg had walked right into his world and made him see that the best was right here. Right now. His mind was reeling to make sense of what she'd said. He had to clarify. He had to make sure he got the facts right. "Are you saying that Eddie had more than just the one affair?"

"Oh, he had an affair going on when we were engaged, I found out later." She looked so lost, and when she shook her head, she pressed her cheek against his palm and he treasured the contact.

He brought his free hand to cradle the other side of her face, holding her, knowing how vulnerable she felt. Because she was somehow in his soul and he couldn't explain it, but he did believe in it.

"I didn't know he was like that. I never really liked him, but I didn't know him." Jared felt confused, he felt angry and he just felt—too much, too furious, but most of all the hard certain punch of one emotion shone through the others, strong enough to light any darkness.

Love.

"Nobody really knew Eddie. I was married to him and I certainly didn't. It was like he had a secret life.

As if he was wearing a costume of a good husband and a good Christian, but when he could step away from that role, he was a horrible man. Calling me on his cell phone saying he was just leaving his office, so I knew when to have dinner on the table, when in truth he was at some cheap motel, renting a room by the hour. I know, because I would find a receipt and confront him."

"A receipt?" Jared ground out between clenched teeth. It was one of the hardest things he'd ever done to hold back his rage. "He did that to you?"

"Constantly." She held herself very still, as if she were a cracked piece of blown glass ready to splinter apart. "What should I have done? The first time I'd been married just a year. I found out about the other affairs much later. He swore it was just that one time. It was a moment of weakness with a secretary who was temping at his office, they just got to working late and were carried away and—"

"He was wrong. There is no excuse." Jared felt boiling hot with fury. "Why didn't you try counseling with Reverend Fraser? Or just leave him?"

"You think I didn't?" Anguish vibrated through her.

And into him. He could feel how empty she felt inside. *So this is what happened. This is what Eddie did.* He'd drained the love right out of her heart. Jared could sense it as sure as the silken softness of her face. As the bleak sound in her sigh.

"He would apologize and he'd promise to do better, and he'd sweet-talk me and court me, and I would finally believe him. I wanted to be loved so badly. But it didn't last, and he'd hurt me again with his lies and his *cheating.*" She grimaced as if that word brought the greatest of pains.

Of course it would. Jared had never been tempted by other women, but even if he had been, he could never have caused Vanessa that deep level of pain. Or Meg.

But she didn't know that, he realized. He could see all the agony of heartbreak and betrayal bottled up inside her. "How could a man do that to you even once?"

"Look at me. I'm too skinny. I'm too good. He constantly said I'm too plain. I wasn't enough." She wheezed out a sound of pure hopelessness. "It was my fault. I did my best, but it just never seemed to last. He fell away from me every time. I couldn't keep his interest. He said he loved me, but—"

"That's not love, Meg."

"You don't understand. Has there ever been a woman who wasn't charmed by you?"

"Yeah, I can think of one." He smoothed windblown wisps of her hair behind her ear. "You."

"Then you'd be wrong." What should have been bitter words came out on a sob, came like a confession on the wind because she knew the answer. And she bit her lip before any more secrets popped out. She needed to keep Jared at a safe distance. To push him away, not draw him close.

So she took a deep breath for self-preservation and said the honest words that she knew he would understand. And respect. "I forgave Eddie every time. No matter how brutally he'd hurt me, he'd just leave my heart in pieces. He is a sweet-talker with a silver tongue, but I didn't see that. I only saw my husband was accusing me of not being a good Christian by not forgiving him. And it made something die inside me each time, but I loved him. I wanted it to work. And how foolish is that?"

"Sweet talk isn't loving talk. And a good Christian forgives, yes, but, Meg, he hurt you."

"I realized too late that I'd made a mistake in marrying him. I promised before God to love him for better or worse. I wanted a happy family, for once, instead of the cold unhappy one I grew up in. I wanted a good marriage. I worked so hard at it. But it didn't work out. I didn't have enough. I just…ran out. There's nothing left inside me. I can't feel my heart. I can't feel anything. I just can't give you what you want, Jared. It's just not in me."

Shame choked her, that this man she'd been rivals with in high school, whom she'd never wanted to show any weakness to, now knew nearly the worst thing about her. Like Eddie, he would use it for his benefit, but he had to understand. There would be no real marriage. No trust. No intimacy. Not even friendship.

There was no way she was ever going to let a man do that to her again. Eddie had cut her deep enough, but if she let her guard down and reached out to Jared, as he kept trying to get her to do, she instinctively knew that he could hurt her all the more. This strange awareness and connection to him, if she was honest with herself, went back over a decade.

She could love him wholly with the innocence and the honesty of that teenaged girl, if she allowed herself, if she had the heart. She would love him so completely, and then how would she fare when the inevitable happened?

Twilight lured the shadows out and the wind from the southeast. A cool gust kicked through the trees, making the leaves rustle and then roar. The chimes clanked discordantly and the aging blooms flew off the petunias and scattered along the patio, faint blots of pink and purple in the waning light.

It was as if the wind beat at her, too, as if she were as withered as those spent flowers and lifted her out of the chair, pushed her past Jared. She hurried into the house, leaving him standing there in the gathering dark. The first pings of rain slammed against the patio and she closed the door and kept going, feeling more alone than she had ever been.

Chapter Fourteen

With a twin in each arm, Jared followed Meg down the walkway to his mom's back door. He was looking forward to tonight's Bible study not only for himself, but also for Meg.

She'd lost more than her relationship with the Lord. A broken heart was a hard thing to mend, but he felt her sadness went deeper. She'd been a wonderful helpmate to him throughout the week. Kind and helpful, she'd washed and ironed his work clothes, kept house with boundless efficiency, made sure the twins had plenty of love and always included him in decision making. It turned out that running the household and parenting the boys came easily. Meg and he made decisions in a similar way, and it was a natural compatibility.

But when she wished him a good day every morning, it was only friendship she offered. She was good to him, but she had no hugs or kisses. No emotional intimacy. She listened to his stories from his day at work and shared her thoughts. She cared. There was no doubt about it. But he wanted more than a helpmate, a coworker. Marriage wasn't a business partnership. It was about trust, commitment and real love.

Still, he had hope. Trust took time and he intended to be a steady rock for her. Their marriage was new and coming on the tail of a painful divorce. He knew they could make this work. He was determined. Because that's what love was—ever faithful and ever constant. It wasn't easy for him to open his heart, either, but when he glanced at her, his soul stirred with affection. He couldn't help loving her, although he had so much at stake, too. The boys' happiness. Failing to be what she needed. Failing to be able to really love again. No, the tough waters of marriage were not easy to negotiate. And his heart, like hers, was at risk.

"Oh, Meg, it's so good to see you!" Mom's loving voice rose like the sweet scents of honeysuckle and climbing roses and, leaning her cane against the door-jamb, made both arms free to give Meg a hug.

He watched as Meg returned the affection and he fell a little bit more in love with her, as the bold evening light streaming through the backyard trees and burnishing her hair like molten fire. He wrestled down the urge to wind his fingers through her hair, to have the right to be with her like a husband with his wife. To share those intimate little smiles. Those little looks that said, "we're together."

"Here are my grandbabies!" Mom's loving voice chimed. "Let me see my boys! Have you grown since I saw you last?"

The twins leaned toward her. Luke called, "Grum!" and Chance said, "Ah!"

Mom's laughter was sheer happiness as she hugged the boys and dispensed kisses to their foreheads and faces.

Meg could have turned toward him and spoke to him with her eyes, something shared between them, but she didn't because there's wasn't a relationship like that... yet. She held the screen door graciously for his mom, who was excited to see her grandchildren, but she was watching the boys try to charm their grandmother instead of sharing the experience with him.

Strangely bereft, Jared knew he had to give it time. But her words kept coming back to him. *I just...ran out. There's nothing left inside me. I can't feel my heart. I can't feel anything. I just can't give you what you want, Jared. It's just not in me.*

Was there no hope for them? Frustrated, he managed to let his mom lift Luke away. Chance squealed to get down, and Jared complied, feeling his heart warm at the twins' happiness. *This is what it's all about,* he reminded himself. Why he and Meg married, before they'd had the luxury of falling in love—so the boys would be happy.

When he'd first proposed, he'd imagined he'd court her after the wedding. Courting, in the sense of spending time getting to know one another. Aside from the challenging work of parenting two toddlers, he figured Mom could pitch in and babysit—she'd offered so many times, he knew she'd be thrilled—and he'd take Meg out to a movie and dinner.

Time together, that's what they needed, or so he'd thought. Flowers, romance, thoughtfulness.

If only those things would work. He and Meg had always had...well, chemistry for lack of a better word. Interest and spark and over a decade hadn't diminished that. But there was a new problem—it was one-sided. His.

"After you, ma'am." He reached high to take the

edge of the screen door and met her direct gaze, so she wouldn't argue. Meg was highly independent and he could sense her dread of entering the house where he held a weekly Bible study and had since his teenage years. She was all out of faith, too, she'd told him, but she'd come.

As she slipped beneath his arm, he caught the gentle floral scent of her perfume, felt the brush of her hair against the underside of his forearm and he swore she took his heart with her as she swept through the doorway and into his mother's country kitchen. She didn't look back. She didn't reach for his hand. She wasn't cold—she just wasn't in a relationship with him.

"Mama! Looky?" Excited, Luke held up his iced cookie in the shape of a caboose and then sank his teeth deep on the back wheel. "Yum!"

"Yum." Chance held up his own cookie.

"Wow. Train cookies." Meg knelt to inspect the intricately decorated cookies. "What is this?"

"'Boose!" Chance got in his answer as Luke shouted "caboose!"

"Good boys." She wrapped an arm around each and snuggled them close, cookies and crumbs and smeared icing forgotten. The marks they left on her designer silk jacket didn't seem to faze her, and he liked that about her as she released them.

Unaware of how lucky they were to have a loving mom, the twins squealed some more and reached for more cookies on the plate that his mother was lowering down for them to pilfer from. He opened his mouth to let Mom know that with that much sugar, the twins wouldn't be able to settle down to sleep until midnight, but the words faded on his tongue as Meg caught his attention and held it.

She was still kneeling, icing marks on both sides of her collar, a piece of cookie crumb on the front curl of her hair. The breeze from the floor vent was stirring her fiery locks, and as she watched Donna interact with the boys, the pure light of love that filled her was beyond breathtaking. Beyond beautiful.

His throat filled, and he couldn't speak for a different reason. Hard shards of emotion seemed to knife in his windpipe and cut every time he breathed. He didn't know why loving someone hurt. Maybe it was the intensity of it, the physical act of a heart expanding, he didn't know.

He only knew that as Meg rose, her tasteful beige set of jacket and shell and slacks caught the light, or maybe it was just the light of his spirit, and he felt more than uplifted. He felt transformed. How did a man fall in love with a woman so many times? And each time more powerful than the last? As he watched, motionless, Meg tugged a wrapped gift from her huge handbag.

Her words came to him like music. "I can never thank you enough for helping my friends with their wedding present for your son and I."

"Oh, dear, how could I not help? It was an inspired idea. Look at them. I hope you don't mind, I intend to spoil them good. I'm not sure just how much interference you want from me, but with their birthday coming up in a few weeks, and you working full-time, I just want you to know, I'm here to help you with whatever you need. I love to bake cakes, in case you need a hint. Oh, and I have—"

Mom was in her element, a loving woman having someone new to dote on, but the look on her face when she spotted the gift in Meg's hand, it stopped her cold. Her eyes filled. "I, ah—"

"This is a little something for you. I thought you might understand."

He didn't know what Meg had done, but he knew her thoughtfulness of a gift meant the world to his mother, who was always doing and giving to others. Mom seemed to melt, if that was possible, and adore Meg even more. She ripped off the fancy ribbons and tore at the tasteful floral paper to reveal two framed photographs and a medium-sized photo album. Jared didn't have to see the pictures Meg had chosen—he already knew. Mom's tears said it all.

Their first family picture taken at the courthouse. And pictures of the boys she'd snapped last night with her digital camera as they played in the backyard. Mom began going on and on, hugging Meg, setting up the framed pictures on top of the living room piano. Other voices joined Mom's and Meg's, but the conversations grew vague and distant as Jared took a step and felt the earth begin to spin beneath his feet. He wasn't fainting. He wasn't dizzy. The back of his neck prickled.

Through the burr of friends gathered in the living room and the merry bells of laughter, he felt a small hand grab him around the knee. He looked down at one blond head, with a familiar out-of-control cowlick sticking straight up from the crown. Luke tipped his head back, eyes wide.

"What is it, little man?"

"Da-dee." With an expressive sigh, the toddler leaned his cheek against Jared's knee, exactly like his Chance but different, too. His son, now, for all time.

And there was his answer, too.

God worked in mysterious ways, there was no doubt. Jared lifted the boy into his arms as the conversations clarified and it seemed like another ordinary evening of Bible study and fellowship. With one shining exception.

"Ah, you have the look of a new husband, that of love."

Jared startled. There, at his side, was Reverend John Fraser. A good man, and Jared couldn't have asked for a better pastor over the years. He thought about all that his minister had done for him after Vanessa's passing. He'd been a rock that Jared could lean on as well as offering some pretty awesome spiritual insight.

God had blessed him in many ways, and Jared would always be grateful for this good father figure in his life. But how did he admit to the man he most admired that this marriage to Meg wasn't what it seemed? That they'd rushed to wed because of the boys, and there were a lot of obstacles to overcome? But any way he looked at it, Meg was a blessing.

So Jared was able to answer honestly. "I am very pleased. I could not have asked for a finer woman for my wife."

"She's certainly a loving mother."

They both turned to watch Meg with the boys, a hand gently placed at the back of each blond head, lightly guiding them into the back part of the house with his mom in the lead. The emotion growing in his chest was more than affection.

"She's great with Chance. Some women might play favorites with her own son, but she's not like that. When I think of all the women Chance's twin could have been placed with, and all the what-ifs of the situations, I can't believe I have Meg. I couldn't have asked for someone better."

"The best answered prayers are the ones we don't

even make," the reverend said sagely. "That's when God peers into our hearts and gives to us what we don't even know to ask for."

"That's exactly how it feels." Jared's throat filled again. But how to heal her heart? An ocean of emotional distance separated him from Meg—an ocean she kept between them on purpose.

Distance she insisted on, even now, in his mother's home when there was only love and fellowship surrounding her, politely retreating to the kitchen to help Mom with the refreshments.

He felt lost. So very lost.

He doesn't realize how deeply painful it is for me to be here. The realization struck her as she searched for her Bible in her oversize bag. She withdrew the worn leather volume, given to her by her father, when he'd been a much less cynical man. The image came with a memory of him coming to tuck her into bed on the rare nights when he wasn't on call, being one of the area's in-demand vascular surgeons.

"I found this in my old things." He sat down, dipping the mattress, his baritone steady and dependable. "It was my mother's. You remember Gramma Victoria? She told me she wanted you to have this."

Even as a grade-school child, Meg remembered her loving grandmother, who'd died over a year before. The grandmother who'd always had time for her. Who never had charity meetings and hospital meetings and parties to dress up for. Gramma Victoria had smelled like roses and sugar cookies. Who'd always worn a cross around her neck, given to her by her husband, who'd died before Meg had been born.

Inside was a handwritten note in Gramma's squiggly printing. "Believe," was all it said, and she'd signed it simply, "Love, Gramma."

As a child, she'd treasured the Bible and believed, as her Gramma had. She'd held so tight to God's word, she'd done her best to love and forgive and do what was right, and it had simply wrung her out. Left her broken. What did a person do when there was nothing left inside to believe with?

"Last time Ramon picked a passage he wanted to talk about, one that I think has a great lesson for the faithful, because, let's face it, faith is not an easy thing. Life tests us with hardship and pain and struggle, and our faith has to be strong enough or what's the alterative?"

We're utterly lost, Meg answered silently.

"The passage is from Romans. 'We also rejoice in our sufferings, because we know that suffering produces perseverance; perseverance, character; and character, hope.'" Jared's leadership wasn't pompous, but honest. "That kind of sounds like to me like we should feel happy to have horrible things happen in our lives. Thanks, God, for the suffering. I needed that."

Knowing comments rose around the circle. Meg felt emotion burn in her throat. Faith was easier in better times. Her reliance on her faith and her belief that God was working for the greater good in her life had kept her together in her marriage. And then, when the final straw broke, when Eddie had told her he was leaving her for someone younger and more fun, she hadn't understood. She'd prayed so hard. She'd worked so hard. She'd given up so much of herself for a marriage that had hurt her.

Maybe that wasn't what God intended love to be. The awareness came as if He had come to whisper in her ear.

She brushed it aside because why else had her marriage before been so bad?

"You all know the dark times I had after Vanessa's death," Jared went on, and his hand covered hers on the leather cover of her grandmother's Bible. "But what we see as tragedy may not be, in another perspective. The feelings are real, believe me. I thought a part of me had died, but it was a benevolent act. Vanessa's body had failed her, and the good Father brought her home instead of allowing her to suffer. Now that I'm through the dark waters of grief, I can see that He strengthened me. He got me through the loss and gave me the chance for a happy future."

Meg looked down at their joined hands. A happy future? How? Romantic love was a myth. A happy marriage a fairy tale. But Jared seemed to believe what he was saying.

Reverend Fraser cleared his throat. "What we have to remember is that God never abandons us. We are his children. Would anything force you to stop loving your children?"

Nothing. Meg felt her heart squeeze when she didn't want to feel anything at all. It was safer. Love brought pain. Trust brought pain. She had to keep afloat for the boys' sake. They deserved a stable home instead of the chaos she'd known with Eddie. But what chaos had there been with Jared? Not yet, anyway.

Reverend Fraser continued. "We all have our times of darkness. There are example after example of this in the Bible. What we have to remember is this. 'Whether you turn to the right or to the left, your ears will hear a voice behind you, saying, "This is the way; walk in it."' You may have to listen very hard, but it is always there."

Meg closed her eyes. She knew both men were right. She was wondering in the dark but she could not hear. There was no voice. No guidance.

"Ma-ma!"

She turned toward her baby's voice, twisting up and out of the chair and away from the circle of fellowship, before she realized it was Chance racing toward her, rubbing his ear with one fisted hand.

Big tears pooled in his eyes. "Ow."

"Come here, baby." She pulled him into her arms, rubbing the back of his head for comfort. His little weight and warmth was so like her Luke's, but she loved this little boy, too, who was also his own little person. He gave a manful sob, struggling not to cry. "I'll help you, little one."

He rubbed his face against her neck, holding on so tight.

Oh, sweet little man. She held him just as tightly back, letting him know he was safe. That she would take care of him now. That no matter what, she'd be here to help ease an earache or wipe away his tears. She kissed his forehead, excused herself from the group and hurried to the kitchen, where Luke sat on the edge of the table, his feet swinging while Donna examined the results of an ear thermometer.

"Oh, not Chance, too!" The lovely elderly lady looked truly distressed. "Luke started rubbing his ear and I whipped him up here to check him out and I just thought Chance was running to you. He considers you his mama now."

"I hope I can live up to that title." Meg couldn't have asked for a more sincere mother-in-law. She was a blessing. And not the only one. Chance held on so tight. And she *felt*, after being numb so long. The ice, like the northern tundra, so high and deep, cracked a little more as she soothed the boy clinging to her.

"I've got some over-the-counter medication," Donna explained as she handed over the thermometer and swept Luke onto her hip. "Do you want to give the pediatrician a call?"

"I'd better. Luke has a history of some pretty stubborn ear infections."

"Chance, too." Donna retrieved the handheld phone and handed it over. There was a caring wreathed into her lovely face and radiating from her like light from the sun.

Meg shied away, not from the woman, but from the closeness she was offering. The ice that had surrounded her heart was dangerously cracked, and if she wasn't careful, if she wasn't strong, she felt as if she would simply crumble apart, like an iceberg shattering and drowning in the vast frigid ocean.

And yet she so longed for the relationship Donna was offering, which made it doubly hard as she turned away. She punched numbers, making the call to the nurse practitioner on duty, who knew Luke and was willing to prescribe for Chance as well. Meg scheduled an appointment for later in the week. It was an efficient call made all in the matter of minutes, and when she clicked off the handset and returned it to the wall-mounted cradle, Donna was still there, gently rocking a whimpering Luke.

"Meg, I'm so glad you and Jared…well, I just mean to say—"

"Hey, how are the little ones?" Jared strolled into the kitchen, strong with purpose, diminishing the size of the large kitchen so it felt as if it were tiny, as if the walls had shrunk and the ceiling had slid downward and she was trapped between the cabinets.

Between Donna's offered kindness and Jared's magnetic charisma or whatever it was, the glacial freeze of her soul warmed. Dangerous, that's what Jared was. Not a charming man with charisma, as Eddie had been, but a concerned father who'd come to check on his sons.

She'd never seen anything more attractive in a man. When he came to her, she felt him in the deepest part of her spirit. It was a terrible wrenching, as painful as if her tender flesh had seared to a subzero metal post and was being ripped away, leaving her raw and open, exposed more than she had ever been before.

It made no sense, but that's how it felt, and she couldn't say why this was happening or how. She only knew she could never let Jared know how he affected her. She could never put her trust in a man again. She could never put her life and her future under a man's control.

She'd learned the hard way to be independent, and that was what she was going to be. If she couldn't hear God, if she couldn't feel Him in her life or in her heart, then she was going to do her best on her own. And that meant staying as alone as possible. But these good people were finding their way into her heart, bit by bit, and she felt as if she were going down for the third time in frigid water.

"Oh, here, let me take him." Jared was talking to his mom.

Meg watched as he transferred Luke into his arms, murmuring low to him. The soothing baritone was caring and rich enough to seem as if it could right any wrong, heal any wound.

Luke gave a watery sob and leaned his cheek against Jared's chest. "Da-dee."

So much emotion rang in that single word. Luke needed Jared. Chance needed Jared. She would do anything for her boys. Anything for her sons. Because that's what they were. She pressed a kiss to Chance's forehead, and his weight was sweet in her arms. This love for the twins was like the faint light in an utterly dark night, the only signal guiding her.

Chapter Fifteen

Jared could read the surprise on Meg's face as easily as the fatigue. It had been a rough last couple of hours. He'd run to the pharmacy and brought back antibiotics.

He made his apologies to the other members of the Bible study—he felt like a heel running out on them since he was the group's leader. But Ben Cavanaugh volunteered to lead on in Jared's absence, and that was a weight off his mind as he loaded the boys into the back seat of his truck.

The boys' earaches were really starting to set in, and he and Meg had two poor crying babies all the way home. They got right to work taking care of the twins. She'd grabbed Luke and rocked him and comforted him in the rocking chair in the boys' room. He took the recliner in the living room, which also rocked, and comforted Chance, who sniffled and sobbed until finally the medicine kicked in and he drifted off to sleep.

For a while Jared held him, just to make sure, before he'd packed the boy down the hall. And he wondered, as he laid Chance carefully into his crib, if he looked as exhausted as Meg did.

He covered up his son with his beloved train blanket. The reverend's words tonight struck home. The image of Chance calling Meg "Mama" and running to her when he was sick said everything.

Heaven couldn't have been any clearer if God had used a bright neon arrow. He loved Meg. He loved that she was the mother Chance had needed. He loved that she'd married him, despite her fears and the heartbreak of her first marriage, so that her son would have a brother. She'd opened up her house and her life, and worked hard to provide and care for the boys, as he did.

No, he could not ask for more. With his heart full, there was only one thing he could do. Just one, because that's what love was. Selfless. "Let me take him, so you can go to bed. You mentioned something about a meeting tomorrow."

"Oh, the big crisis client is back but needs a meeting. My guess is that it will get rescheduled for later in the week—he's not the most reliable at keeping his appointments. But if he does, I've worked just fine with little sleep before, trust me. I know what truly matters." Wearily she pressed a kiss to the back of her son's head while he slept, limp against her shoulder.

"Meg, so do I."

His words couldn't have touched her more, and she could only stare up at him, wondering if he was real. Or was he some figment of her tired mind and most of her lifetime of wishful thinking? Like a dream man, he lifted Luke from her arms and settled the sleeping boy, who began to stir, against his wide chest.

"Go to bed. I'll watch over our boys."

Our boys. How did she tell him how wonderful that sounded? It was the only thing she could hold on to. "You have work tomorrow, too, and you're leaving on Saturday. I know you don't have much time to spare."

"And you do?"

She didn't know what to say to that. Her mind was foggy, her back hurt, her head ached and fatigue crackled in her arms and legs and made her eyelashes heavy. "I'm used to staying up with Luke. I may as well watch over both of them. You go to sleep."

"I take it Eddie wasn't much of a help to you?"

"He felt it was my duty. And I—" There was no sense hiding pain. The divorce was over, the marriage nothing but a bad memory. "He was never interested in being a real father. It wasn't until we were in the lawyers' offices divvying up our assets when I learned he'd never wanted to adopt, not really. He felt it was sort of an act of contrition. And, I suspect, that if I were busy with a new baby then I wouldn't notice his indiscretions."

"I don't understand. How could anyone not want to love and protect these boys?" Jared's face flushed but it was the only indication that he was angry. He remained steady and calm, his hand splayed on Luke's back, caressing in a slow soothing circle as the boy drifted back to sleep.

"It's all I want."

"That's why you're high on my list. You go on and get to bed. It's after midnight. You can still get six hours if you hurry. And no, don't argue—" He was tender as he brushed a kiss along the side of her cheek—a chaste kiss—and there was nothing objectionable to it.

Except, somehow, it was more than a chaste kiss. It

was affection and longing all mixed up with duty and friendship and she was wise enough to know there was more meant by this small brush of his lips to her cheek—his promise. He wanted a real marriage. And she did not.

The rocking chair groaned slightly when he sat in it, but it was a loud shocking sound in the utter silence of the house. Jared seemed not to notice as he began to rock with Luke slack against him, his little hands resting on Jared's chest.

"I don't absolutely have to be at work until nine, even as late as ten," he was saying. "So I may as well take the boys tonight. You can get the next one. Maybe you won't have a pressing meeting, and I will. We'll work it out, Meg."

"But it doesn't feel right to just leave you with everything."

"That's what I'm right here by your side for. To be right here to help out. To pitch in. We do this together, Meg. This is my turn. It's all right. Do you want me to pick you up and carry you to bed?"

"No, but—" How did she tell him it wasn't only about her guilt over leaving him with the sick boys? The reason she couldn't seem to take a step toward the door was simple. He was breaking through to her deepest core.

When she expected him to be a typical man, or at least, she had to admit, her version of one, he had to go and surprise her. To show her he was better than that. Better than she would ever expect him to be.

And he was killing her, too. Because he was wonderful and any woman would fall for him. It would be so easy to love him. All she would have to do was open her heart and believe in something that she knew did not exist. If only she was as naive as she'd once been. When she believed that happily-ever-afters could happen to a lonely girl who'd grown up in a household of strangers too busy to sit down for a family supper every night.

If she let Jared take care of the boys tonight, then she would have to admit he was even more than wonderful. That she could just simply fall in love with him. That she could come to care about him—and it wasn't going to happen. She wasn't about to let it. She had what was left of her heart and she had to protect it. She wanted what was best for the boys, and that wouldn't be a roller-coaster ride of emotional trauma that went hand in hand with "love."

Or at least that's what she told herself, what she was ready to argue against and strengthen her resolve, but what did Jared have to go and do? He made everything worse. Simply, irrevocable. Totally worse.

"I'm grateful you are here in my life," he said with all the sincerity in the world. "I give thanks everyday for you. That such an incredible woman is my wife."

Utterly overwhelmed, Meg fought against an iceberg of feelings she could not face. That she could not expose.

"Good night," was all she could manage to say before she slipped out into the hall, careful to make as little noise as possible for the sleeping boys.

Never had a night seemed so utterly bleak. Nor had she ever felt so totally alone.

It didn't get better. She woke after a few restless hours and crawled from her bed. After slipping on a lightweight robe over her pajamas, she eased down the hall, her bare feet nearly silent on the carpet runner that led her to the small beacon of light at the end of the corridor. She couldn't say why she paused in the darkness just out of the light's reach, but it was as if she could sense the danger, not of pain or hurt of fear, but of something far more scary.

Jared sat in the halo of the small lamp from the table near his elbow, with Luke slack against his chest, both man and boy sound asleep, breathing softly. It was something she'd never seen before. A strong capable man, smart and talented with a time-consuming career, sleeping in a chair with a child in his arms. It was hard to reconcile the award-winning, world-traveled reporter with the domestic father figure slumbering in the too-small chair.

His neck was crinkled at an awkward angle—he was going to have a stiff neck when he woke up—but he had fallen asleep that way anyway, for Luke's comfort. Never had she seen a man so devoted to his children. Surely her father had taken such little time with her; she had no memory of falling to sleep in her father's arms.

And Eddie, why, he'd rarely changed a diaper much less stayed up to rock a sick baby. I have work in the morning, he'd say.

But Jared? He'd said the perfect thing. He'd offered to let her sleep. If she'd closed her eyes and reached down into her deepest being, deep enough past the wounds and scars and numbness, there was still a tiny, vulnerable place that felt. That dreamed. And there, she knew with certainty, she had wished for a husband like Jared long ago, when Eddie had failed her for the umpteenth time. The image of the man she'd wished Eddie would become was never there.

It was here.

How does a dream come true, even if you'd stopped believing it? Even if you've stopped wanting it?

It is no dream, the wounded places within her reminded her. *This is all the same. Wishing for what can never be. Projecting wishes onto other people. People can never be what you want them to be or what you need.* That was just a cold, hard fact or life. In this world, people watched out for themselves.

And if she wanted to believe there could be more in life, how could she? When she couldn't feel past the wreckage of her own heart? When she feared the God she'd always loved and believed in was nothing but a great big silence? When she was endlessly adrift on a freezing black ocean with no shore in sight?

"Meg." Jared started awake, softly, as if part of his unconscious mind had been keeping tabs on the sleeping toddler in his arms. "Hey, I think this little guy is doing better. How's Chance?"

"Sleeping like a log."

"Looks as if they both ducked a bad bout of this. Chance has been up more nights in pain than I can stand thinking out. I always feel so helpless."

"Exactly."

Their gazes locked. How could it be they had so much in common? Understanding exactly how rough those nights had been, powerless to take away the hurt for a sick baby, Meg swore she could feel the rake of pain like talons in her chest. How easy it would be to lean closer instead of taking a step back to safety. Toward the darkness.

"I just had to check on them." She couldn't stop the strong steel of devotion. "Jared, this is no time to talk about this, but we're in this together, for the duration, right?"

"For the long haul. I'm not going to ever walk away from these kids. And that means I will never walk away from you, either. You're their mother, Meg. They need you so much. Whatever reassurance you need, then fine, let me know. We're already crossing the point of no return for us. We either figure this out or pretty soon or it will be too late. The problems will be too big and we'll never have a chance at anything bigger and better. For us. For the boys."

How many times did she have to tell him? She bit her lip, because the boys were asleep and this was not the time or place. She knew that Jared was trying to comfort her, not start a painful discussion she didn't even want to have. "The boys are better off just like this."

"They are doing better together." Jared stood with care, cradling Luke so as not to wake him. The shadows seemed to emphasize the solid planes of him, how tall he was, how capable.

With powerful tenderness, he settled the sleeping child in his crib and moved to reach for the covers. But Meg was there, automatically at his side, as the shadows were growing darker. At least the boys were feeling better, that's all that mattered, and she was grateful for their comfort as they slept—the harmonious, barely discernable rhythm of their breathing accompanied her to the door.

Ignoring Jared, she reached to pull the door closed behind her, and he was there, his big hand engulfing the brass knob and joining her in the hallway, where only the faint bluish glow of the train-themed nightlight illuminated Jared's silhouette.

It was too dark, but she didn't need to see to know what emotions were playing on his face. She could feel them like the sweep of a mighty ocean wave moving through her until she was filled with it.

Like a warm tropical current unleashed in an arctic sea, and the shock of it left her breathless and confused. She was dazed as he took her by the hand and twined his thicker fingers between hers. He led her down the hall, taking her where she didn't want to go.

Yet her feet kept moving forward, letting him lead the way to the kitchen where Mercy gave a groan as she stretched on the seat cushion and Buster was a dark lump snoring on his bed by the hearth. Jared had fit into her life so neatly. The animals were adjusting, the boys were bonding and she and Jared seemed to parent seamlessly together, as if they were two pieces made to be whole, and that couldn't be possible.

She wouldn't let it be possible. The warmth of his love kept lapping through her like a Caribbean undertow, pulling her where she didn't want to go, melting at the ice that was her heart. What would she do when it was gone? When it broke apart and liquefied and there was nothing left at all? Because that's what marriage did. That kind of love sucked a woman dry. It had happened to her mother. It had nearly happened to her, and thank goodness Eddie chose to leave when he did, because she had nothing more, nothing left to forgive with.

Nothing left to try with. Just enough to get through the day and to be a decent mom. She couldn't lose it. She could feel the iceberg within her beginning to diminish, and like those documentaries where great chunks broke off and slipped away forever into the fathomless water, there was a part of her that was breaking apart, breaking wide open and she couldn't stand the pain.

She wrenched her fingers from Jared's and twisted away, her ears roaring and her pulse pounding with the need for self-preservation. For her to protect enough of herself to keep going on. For the twins' sake.

But Jared didn't understand. He stood there, a hallmark of masculine kindness that was like nothing she'd seen before. His big frame was nothing but an invincible shadow behind the breakfast bar counter and then the small light over the sink flooded on and tumbled across his dark thick hair and dear, handsome face and his weight lifter's shoulders and he was filling the teapot.

He was making her tea? At nearly two-thirty in the morning? No man was that good. No husband that caring. And so what was he trying to do? Lure her into believing the impossible so she would cling to that, as if that were the way things ought to be, so she would put her faith and her heart into something that couldn't exist?

The moment she began to rely on him, to trust he was the kind of man who would make her tea when she was breaking apart inside, who would sit with her and comfort her in the rain, who would stay up to take the last night shift with sick little boys so she could sleep, why, then it would vanish.

She was all out of faith. She'd used it all up. And she wasn't a fool. She turned away, intending to go right back to the boys' room and let Jared make his tea. Whatever. It wasn't going to change the fact of life. Of marriage. Of what a woman could expect from a man who'd placed a ring on her finger. She knew what mattered. The boys.

And Jared, he was their father, but that was all.

That's all she could let him be.

And then, he was there, his hand at her elbow, and without words he knew. How, she didn't know, but she couldn't bear it. She didn't want his pity or his compassion or his love that would push at her and pull at her like a hurricane at sea, leaving her a wreck and lost and drowning.

She broke free, but still it felt as if he were touching her, holding her, offering her what she did not want.

"Let me go," she begged, keeping her voice low so she wouldn't disturb the boys at the end of the hall, but with enough force so that Jared would understand. "Your shift is over. You go ahead and get some sleep. I'll keep an eye on the little ones."

"I told you, I have a more flexible schedule tomorrow."

"But you have a trip to get ready for."

"I might put it off."

Had she heard him right? She could only stare at him. "You want to put off your trip? I thought it was this big assignment you'd been waiting for."

He lifted one shoulder. "It is. But if I have to, I'll pass. You and the twins come first."

She didn't know if he was telling the truth—he looked sincere. Sounded sincere. Felt sincere. And yet, that didn't make a bit of sense with what she knew about him.

How else had he gotten to be a big-shot reporter if he hadn't made a lot of personal sacrifices? "The boys are going to be fine. I'll make sure of it. There's no reason to give up this trip."

"You and the twins are every reason."

How did she get him to see the truth? What either of them might want from a marriage, just simply couldn't be. It didn't exist. It was futile to do this to her. He didn't know that he was destroying her. Until this moment, she'd never known kindness could cut with just as sharp an edge as anger. "This can't go any further."

"What can't?"

"This. This thing between us." Maybe that's why it was so easy for him to be kind and affectionate and want an involved relationship. It wasn't his very being that felt at stake. "Can you feel it?"

"You feel this, too?"

Her eyes widened with surprise. "Then you know how powerful it is and I can't. I just can't—"

"It's more than attraction, Meg, it's more than the friendly relationship you want. I can feel you here, right here in my heart, and I don't know why. I only know that I do. It's like the sun comes out from behind the blackest of storm clouds whenever you come near. It's as if I'm finally alive for the first time, every time I see you."

"Stop it. This can't go on. Don't you know what this is doing to me?"

Jared's heart wrenched at her agony rushing through him, as if it were his own. He remembered her confession from their last big discussion. *There's nothing left inside me. I can't give you what you want, Jared. It's just not in me.* So much pain, his poor Meg. What a good heart she had, that it went so deep and felt so much. It was why she was a great mom and why she was a good wife…they just had some things to iron out. Or at least, that's what he'd believed, but the truth was that as he felt the wave of sadness so bleak, it was like a night without moon or stars or end.

He fell even more in love with his Meg. "There's no need for you to be hurting like this, baby. Whatever Eddie did to you—and I'm sorry for it—but it's over. You're with me now."

"For the boys, that's all. If not for Chance and Luke, I would never have married you. I feel that way today. I'll feel that way ten years from now." Her voice vibrated with anguish and she straightened her shoulders and stood as tall as she was able, like a brave warrior ready to face a battle she could only hope to win.

But she was going to fail. He knew it. His love for her, so warm and uplifting, had brought his spirit back to full life again. "You are nothing short of amazing to me, Meg. To my life. Can't you see how lucky we are? What a blessing we've been given, if we just reach out to one another and believe?"

"That's just it. I don't believe. In love. In blessings. In anything. Not even you."

"You don't mean that. You can't."

"I've never been more sure of anything." She sounded so cold, but it wasn't meanness that drove her to step back, pulling far away from him so that, as she retreated into the hallway, she was lost to him in the darkness. "I don't love you, Jared. Not now. Not ten years from now."

"That's not true." Couldn't she see that he could help her? That he could save her from this horrible pain within her? "I know you love me. I know you do."

"Why? Because you're so fantastic? Because you're so sure any woman could?" She was sobbing, and he knew her words were meant to drive him away.

He couldn't let it work. He couldn't let her win. This wasn't a battle, with enemies on either side. They were a team, they were married, they were together side by side. "You can't lie to me, Meg. You forget. I can feel you right here in my soul. I won't give up on you. I won't stop loving you. I am faithful and true."

"Jared, you have to stop pushing me. You gave your word to me. You said you wouldn't do this to me. That you wouldn't expect—"

"I said I would at least be a friend and a partner to you. But you feel this. You know this is the real thing—"

"You want it to be. I don't love you. How many times do I have to say it?" Meg could feel the last of her heart sliding away, like the last piece of an ancient glacier, and there was nothing but a final splash and darkness. And emptiness where there was no pain, no substance. She couldn't even feel the icy waters of her soul as she turned her back on Jared—and love and his promises and his best intentions because there were no such things. They were as transitory as dust in the wind and she was already blowing away.

She would not bank her sons' futures on a foundation that would blow away. No matter how much it broke what remained of the melted waters of her heart, she stepped into her bedroom alone and closed the door. An image remained of Jared standing as if lost in the darkness, head down, shoulders braced as if against a great pain.

She would give nearly anything—if she had it—to spare him. But there was no comfort for either of them as the night lengthened. She waited for what seemed like forever in the dark and silence until she heard the faint creak of a board in the hallway and, finally, the click of his door shutting.

Only then did she risk slipping down the hall to take her turn with the twins. They were slumbering soundly, but there would be no sleep for her.

Chapter Sixteen

If not for Chance and Luke, I would never have married you. I feel that way today. I'll feel that way ten years from now.

He couldn't keep Meg's words from replaying over and over in his head like a CD stuck on repeat. All through the long commute from Chestnut Grove, it troubled him. Over and over, and nothing, not even his work, would purge her confession from his mind.

There was no possibility of love growing between them.

None.

Here he was, swiping sweat off his brow in a stuffy courtroom stuck in the back corner where no air-conditioning was ever going to find him. It was one of the biggest murder trials in the state in over a decade, and he'd done his background work. He'd interviewed the victims' families, and had come partly on their request, for he'd done his best to be fair and empathetic on the earlier articles he'd done on Prina and his victims.

It was going to be a long trial, he lamented. Longer

because he couldn't seem to pay attention. All he could think about was his wife. *I don't love you. How many times do I have to say it?* Her words had made an irreparable hole in the middle of his chest. The pain only got worse with every passing minute and promised to continue on until it engulfed him.

He realized he loved her completely, down to his soul, and he hadn't realized the risk. He'd been so sure with God on his side that Meg would get over the pain of her first marriage. That she'd succumb to the great plans he had in mind—to court her. Not that he'd gotten around to it in the one very busy work week they'd had together.

And now it was too late.

I don't believe. In love. In blessings. In anything. Not even you. Her confession haunted him.

"The court is now in session," the bailiff announced, and still, Jared could not focus on the work at hand. Grief clawed at him, and it was a bitter thing, to have lost the chance to love…and there was nothing for him to do about it but to accept it. To stop putting Meg through the pain of having to tell him one more time that she would never love him.

Since the client had rescheduled, as she'd predicted, Meg had stayed home with the twins. They were napping, and the house was quiet as the sunlight through the sheers shone softly on the western side of the house and into her eyes, as she took a pound of hamburger from the freezer to defrost. She set the frozen package in the mcrowave and hit the defrost setting before she reached up and twisted the mini blinds closed, blocking out the blinding light. That had to be why her eyes were tearing.

No, it was the emotional residue of last night hanging on her like a stubborn cold. It was the look on Jared's face, one of defeat, as he'd walked out the door. If only there had been a way to fix it. If only there was a way to make things right between them. But what? Jared wanted the impossible from her. There was nothing left in her heart. No love to give him.

The silence seemed to swell around her and she switched on the TV mounted beneath the cabinets. She listened to a talk show host dispense relationship advice while she searched through the pantry shelves. Yeah, right, she thought as she spotted the bag of egg noodles and dug them out from behind a cereal box.

Wasn't that the substance of daytime television— keep searching for true love, you'll find it? And wasn't that a lost cause, selling impossible dreams to women? If her hands weren't full, she'd turn it to something more realistic—or enlightening, she thought, as she nudged the pantry door closed with her foot.

One of the Richmond news anchors broke into the show—a polished, professional looking Hispanic woman who looked grim. "We have breaking news to tell you about. This afternoon the courthouse is under lockdown and the SWAT team has been called to the scene to end a hostage situation. Two men with bombs strapped to their chests interrupted the opening arguments of Christoff Prina's murder trial and have demanded his release—"

Jared is covering that trial. A cold wave of fear slammed into her. The soup cans dropped from her hands and hit the floor, rolling to smack against the base of the cabinets. She gripped the counter for support.

No, he couldn't be in there. He had to be all right.

The news people were probably exaggerating the situation, isn't that what they did for ratings?

"Two hostages have been released," an on-the-scene reporter was explaining with the cordoned off courthouse in the background. "An elderly man who was believed to have had a mild heart attack, and a cameraman who'd been injured by the hostage takers and is said to be in critical condition on the way to an area hospital—"

A cameraman, not a reporter. It couldn't be Jared who was injured. The icy wash of relief was replaced by another realization. Did that mean Jared was still inside? No, he couldn't be. The reporter was saying people in the packed courtroom said many had escaped during the confusion, before the doors were sealed by Prina's men. Surely Jared was one of them. He'd call her any second on his cell to let her know he was all right—

The phone jingled cheerfully on the counter, right on cue. See? She snatched up the receiver. "Jared. I've got the TV on, and—"

"This isn't Jared, Mrs. Kierney." The solemn baritone wasn't a voice she recognized. "This is Todd, your husband's boss."

Why was this man calling her instead of Jared? "Oh, he's busy covering the story, of course. I have the TV on—"

"No, I wanted you to hear this from me instead of from someone else, maybe even on the live television report. Jared was inside the courtroom and he hasn't reported in. We've lost contact with him."

"But his cell phone—"

"Not responding. I'm sorry to tell you this over the phone, but I thought you'd like to know. The second we hear from him, you'll be the first to know."

"Th-thank you." She sank to the middle of the floor, reaching to click off the handset when she heard him continue to speak.

"I'll be praying for him."

Me, too. But there was nothing inside her to feel with. To pray with. Defeated, she thought of the Bible study passage and hoped Jared was right. Jared said that God listened no matter what. Months ago when her soul had felt as frozen as the cold winter day when she'd walked away from her Richmond home, she'd closed her heart to God as surely as she'd done to Eddie. And now that she'd grieved the loss of her marriage, survived a bitter divorce and was rebuilding her life, He was still missing from her heart. She waited and listened. Hoped and prayed.

Nothing. And she needed Him. She'd been wrong to turn away, she'd been overwhelmed and had nothing inside to reach out to the Lord with. But it was no excuse and she was alone. She feared God had abandoned her for good.

Overwhelmed, she was alone and had run out of faith, but she realized she had something that strengthened her. She hadn't realized it, but she was positioned in the kitchen so that she could see straight down the hall. To where a shaft of sunlight, softened by the slats in the blinds, seemed to guide her thoughts.

For the twins' sake she closed her eyes and prayed. *Please, Father, protect Jared. The boys need him. And I—*

The truth, Meg, a little voice demanded. *Tell the truth.*

"I love him. I don't want to, but I do!" Those fateful words made her drown even more. Too much sadness, too much hopelessness, it pulled her down like an undertow until she could not breath. Until there was only the frigid water rising through her, spilling out into silent tears. *Please, let him be all right,* she prayed, because there was nothing else to hold on to, no one else who could possibly help. It felt like a shot in the dark.

There was no answer.

Only the voice of the reporter rising in volume with his alarm. "It sounds like gunfire… No, I'm told it's not the SWAT team. It seems to be coming inside the courtroom, although the question of how they got weapons past security—"

Hopeless, Meg let the phone slip to the floor and buried her face in her hands. She'd been wrong when she'd thought her heart was gone. That there was nothing left of it. She'd thought a heart had limits. That with so much pain, so much betrayal, and it broke. Sometimes so deep and irrevocable that there was no way of putting it back together again.

No, she realized as her heart, that had been whole after all, broke all over again.

Jared was prepared. He'd known there was going to be a bloody end to this conflict—hopefully, the innocent would be spared. Sweat ran in rivulets down his face. The power and ventilation had been cut off to the floor, a standard negotiation technique, and he knew by the growing tension of Prina's men that there was trouble.

Beside him, the court reporter was sobbing silently, her face pressed to the floor, as they had all been ordered to do. She was praying for her children—he could hear her nearly silent words.

I've been ready for You for a long time. Jared found

his thoughts turning heavenward. Ever since Vanessa's passing he'd realized how brief this earthly life was.

And how merciful eternity. He wasn't afraid to die. He was sad to leave the boys. And Meg... He knew she would take incredible care of their twins. He was deeply thankful for her, although she would never have the chance to know it. She would never have the opportunity to be loved the way she deserved—only the way that he could love her. Wholly and fully, for true love could heal all things.

He never saw the sniper. There was only a silent pop, a shattering of ceiling tiles and the first of Prina's men slid bonelessly to the ground. The second cried out, and when he went down his homemade explosive device was beeping. Counting down.

That's when Jared knew he had escaped death. That even as the police were kicking open the doors and shouting orders to evacuate, the timer was clicking down. Experts moved in to try to disarm it, but Jared calmly helped the woman beside him to her feet. He extended his hand to another woman, who was the grandmother of one of the victims, and got her on her feet and headed to the exit.

The bomb squad was working, the police were frantically herding the freed people down the hall, and Jared joined them, feeling time slip into slow motion and stretch into a strange awareness. Life was too short to spend it unhappy. To waste a day without living it fully.

He'd learned that from Vanessa's death. He didn't want Meg to learn that from his.

Chapter Seventeen

~

I never should have said those things to him. Regret weighed like a two-ton anchor around her neck. It was the only emotion she could feel. Otherwise she was as numb as freezing water. It was as if her heart had fractured utterly, leaving nothing to feel any emotions with. Last night, she'd lashed out at Jared and she wished she could take it all back. She wished she'd had the courage of heart to have opened up.

It was too late. And now Jared could be dead and never know how she felt. Never know that she'd found her way to the shore. To him.

She realized she was still holding onto the phone. Woodenly, she crossed the kitchen and fit the handset into the cradle, and had to move her bag out of the way. The shoulder strap had fallen over the contacts of the cradle's chargers. Something caught her eye—her grand-mother's Bible. The age-worn pages of the book were soft as satin against her fingers as she lifted it into the light.

The feel of the expensive paper and the tangible

presence of the Lord's words used to, at one time, comfort her through dark hours—or so it had seemed. She opened the cover, letting the worn old leather brush her fingertips and there was her Gramma Victoria's handwriting. *Believe.*

It was like taking steps on solid land after being washed out from the sea. How great it felt to stand, to feel the solid foundation beneath her feet. She hugged the Bible to her chest, and everything clicked into place, like a key in a rusty lock. She'd fallen away, and she'd doubted God, but God had not left her alone. He'd stood by her, holding her up when she was drowning, carrying her to shore when she could not swim.

Even now He was here as the phone rang and caller ID said it was a friend of Jared's from Bible Study, and the doorbell rang and it was Donna, stumbling in, the mother she'd always wished her own mother could be.

And suddenly she realized there was a man standing in the doorway. A tall man with a linebacker's shoulders and a crooked grin that made her soul breathe and her spirit shine and her heart renew. True love could do that, or so she'd heard from a very reliable source.

And he was running toward her—no, racing as if he were sprinting for an Olympic gold, and she was running, too. She flew into his arms. He was solid, he was real, and he was hers. His kiss was not a tender kiss, but one of gratitude and longing and joy. Her husband had come home, safe and sound, the man she loved beyond measure. She wrapped her arms around him, sank against the steeled plane of his chest and held on with all her strength.

Hot molten tears swelled upward, burning her eyes. "Jared, I thought I might never see you again. I thought—"

"I know—me, too, but I'm right here, baby." His lips brushed her forehead and then her temple. Healing and demanding kisses that were not like anything she'd ever felt before. Devotion and tenderness seemed to radiate from him and into her.

"What if you hadn't come back?" She pressed her cheek against his chest, savoring the sound of his heartbeat, the warm solid feel of him and the feelings within her that were more than friendship could ever be. More than respect. More than love.

She'd found her heart, she was walking on solid ground and she was no longer blind to the truth of her life. She could see the blessings surrounding her and the love like a gentle light from God who had brought her home. "I love you so much, my dear, sweet husband."

The surprise jolted through him, and he cupped her chin with the warm steel of his hand. "What did you say?"

"I love you more than I thought possible. When I saw the news report, I knew you were in that courtroom, and realized I could lose you. And my heart just broke all over again."

Sobs shredded her, but it wasn't like before. This love she had with Jared didn't tear her into pieces. It didn't diminish her.

"If anything had happened to you—I know I said I never would, but you are my heart, Jared. I...I l-love you." She held on so tight, not even the sobs that ripped through her could overpower the truth of her confession. "I don't want to, but I can't stop this from happening."

"It's called love, true and stalwart and unconditional. The same way I love you." His words fanned against the top of her head, mildly ruffling her hair, and his arms banded around her, unyielding iron. "You don't have to be afraid. The past is over, and I'm here now. Right where I'm going to stay."

"I hurt you."

"You did, but I forgive you." He stroked his hand along the line of her jaw, savoring the delicate line of her face and cheek. "That's what real love is. Do you see that now?"

"You should be furious with me. Those things I said—"

"You were hurting. Besides, my love for you is so strong, words can't break it. Other people can't destroy it. Death won't end it." He wound his fingers into her thick lustrous curls. "'Love is patient, love is kind. Love is not jealous, it does not brag, and it is not proud…it always trusts, always hopes, and always remains strong. Love never ends.' That's how I love you."

"And how I love you," she said.

Her hair caressed his knuckles like fine silk. As she leaned into his touch, he knew things were going to be better. That they were going to be better. "Do you finally have faith in me?"

"I believe in you. In the man I've come to know." She'd been lost for so long, but the truth was, she'd never known what real love was before. She hadn't grown up in a loving family. When she'd married Eddie, she hadn't realized his easy flattering charm was not love.

This was. Steady as a lighthouse's fiery beam and powerful enough to shine through even the fiercest storm life had to offer. She held Jared tight and gave silent thanks to the Lord who, when she was lost, had brought her home.

Epilogue

Three weeks later

Sunshine drifted gently through the stained-glass windows of the Chestnut Grove Community Church, casting jeweled light on the couple standing before the altar. The bride's rich red curls were pulled up into a knot, and flowers and pearls graced her wispy tendrils beneath the exquisite veil. She wore a princess-style wedding dress that shone like the rarest of pearls.

At her side was her groom, proud to be there in his black tux. The way he held her hand through the ceremony and couldn't take his eyes off her told of how deep his love and how fathomless his devotion.

When Reverend Fraser pronounced them husband and wife, their close family and friends breathed a sigh of wonder at the tender affection, so pure and bright, as Jared Kierney lifted his wife's veil and before God and witnesses kissed his beloved the way a woman would dream of being kissed—tenderly, respectfully and endlessly sweet.

But there was a glimmer in the groom's eyes that

made her blush, for there was a reception at the Hamilton Hotel before they could spend their wedding night together alone. They walked down the aisle and into the affirming brightness of the sun as handfuls of silken pink petals rained down from the well-wishers lining the path. A gleaming limousine was waiting, the air-conditioning a welcome relief from July's heat, but not as appreciated as the privacy.

As the car pulled away from the curb, she snuggled into her husband's arms. Romance did exist, and it was so incredibly sweet. "I'm so glad you wanted to renew our vows."

"See how well my ideas work out?"

Oh, he was far too sure of himself. "Sometimes you do come up with a few good ones," she conceded.

"A few? I'm the one who came up with the idea to get married in the first place."

"And what a good idea that was." Happy. That's what her life had been since she'd opened up her heart again. To life. To love. To Jared. There was no more sadness. Just the comforting joy of sharing her life with him. Of raising their sons together.

"Too bad you didn't ask me ten years ago."

"Hey, are you saying I should have proposed in high school?"

"You could have asked me out back then. Something tells me we would have still ended up together in a limousine, on the way to our wedding reception."

"God works in mysterious ways. After all the heartache we've both been through, He saw us safely here."

"Even when I was lost. I am so grateful He led me to you."

"Me too, darlin'." Jared kissed her hand, a loving gesture that made her soul fill with more love for this man. "Have I told you today how much I love you?"

"Only about a dozen times. That's not nearly enough."

His eyes twinkled with trouble, and dimples dug into his cheeks as he leaned closer. "There's telling. And then there's showing."

His kiss was a promise of all the good things to come. The sharing and affection and intimacy, as the car eased to a stop in front of the Hamilton Hotel. Inside would be a small reception with the people in their lives who mattered the most.

And from this day on, life would be its own celebration. Their future together glittered as happily as the sunshine on the fountain in front of the hotel. She intended to treasure her life with Jared and their boys, because nothing was as precious as this gift of love. She felt blessed as she laid her hand in Jared's and stepped out into the bright, beautiful world.

The clink of his tool bags echoed in the coved entry of the Tiny Blessings building. Ben Cavanaugh had done so many repairs and renovations on this old cranky building, that he spotted right away a few more to-do's to add to his list. It was a fine Monday morning and it promised to be a hot one. He was more than glad to make his way inside and let the old cooling system wheeze over him.

The scent of freshly brewed coffee greeted him in the reception area, but no one was in yet. The wall clock read twenty minutes to eight. He knew Kelly was in because he'd seen her car in the parking lot. She hadn't heard him or she would have popped out to say hello.

"Hey, Kelly." He didn't want to startle her, so he waited.

There came a distant thump, but no Kelly. That wasn't right, so he headed back, calling out her name.

With every step past the neat but empty desks, his concern grew. "Kelly? Are you all right back here?"

"Oh! Ben!" She tumbled out of a narrow closet, cobwebs clinging to the front of her tailored suit jacket and caught in her blond hair. "You startled me. I couldn't hear a thing."

"We've been friends for a long time. I've never known you to spend a lot of time in closets. Is there anything you need help with? A lightbulb to change or file cabinet to move?" he asked with a smile.

Her gaze zeroed in on his tool bag. "You are a Godsend. Bring your hammer and follow me."

"Into the closet?" He did as he was told. She didn't seem to be kidding. Kelly Young was a serious woman and this was apparently no exception. He squeezed through the narrow door into the tiny area where old shelves with blistering paint lined two walls. Files and dusty, forgotten banker's boxes lined the shelves from the floor to the ceiling. File cabinets crowded the other wall and ate up most of the floor space.

"Back here." Kelly had squeezed between the last file cabinet and the end of the shelving. "I accidentally knocked against it when I was moving the file cabinets—"

"Why are you moving the file cabinets?"

"There have been a lot of old records that Pilar, Anne and I have found. You know the Kierney twins?"

"I do. Wasn't that some wedding? You didn't come sit by me. I could've used the company."

"You poor thing. Now come here and help me move this."

"No please or anything?" He grinned, because he was only joking with her. He thought the world of Kelly and was glad to call her his friend.

"You push and I'll pull." He took the harder task,

hooking his hammer on the end of a shelf, so he could use both hands. He grabbed the side of the file cabinet and heaved. The unbelievably heavy contraption groaned and squeaked and hopped until it was over far enough that Kelly gave him a nod. "What do you need me to do? Build more shelves?"

"No, I want you to demolish this wall." She rapped her knuckles against the painted plywood. The hollow ring had Kelly nodding. "I was getting the boxes down from the top shelf and one of them fell against this wall. That's how I noticed it sounds hollow behind it. I think it's a false wall."

"That's how you got dust in your hair." Ben stepped back. "You know, it's not uncommon for old structures like this that are renovated over centuries to be partitioned up. It's probably just dead space."

"Except that there's something in there." She snatched up his hammer and offered it to him.

He recognized that glint in her pretty eyes. "Fine. But you'll see that I'm right."

"I'm not wrong about this."

She could feel it in her bones. Ever since Meg and Jared had walked into this office with their identical little boys, her suspicions had been right. Every one. She'd started back a year ago when Barnaby Harcourt had been in charge and chronologically searched every record. At first there were small errors, then more suspicious ones. If twins could be adopted separately and their records falsified, then what else would she find?

Dust flew and she covered her ears as he went to work. She backed out of his way, it was a very small closet. The demolition sounds reverberated through the tidy office as she checked on the coffeemaker—the coffee was ready. She'd made it herself, not wanting to wait for fellow early-bird Pilar to get in and make it. She filled two cups. By the time she returned, Ben had stopped banging.

"Hey, there *is* something back here." Down on one knee, he was sliding the freed wall panel to the side. It moved easily, as if it were made to, and revealed more shelves. Only two boxes of records were tucked in the small space, but Kelly had put down the coffee and joined Ben on the floor on autopilot.

He heaved the first box out, and then left her to her work. It was labeled 1970-1975 in bold block lettering she recognized as Barnaby Harcourt's. What was the former director trying to hide? There was no possible way this was simply storage space for more records. In fact, she'd already been through the adoption paperwork from the early- to mid-seventies. She'd found her parents' names on a file folder, because they'd adopted her from this agency thirty-five years ago.

She swiped at the thick layer of dust on the box lid. Obviously no one had looked at these records in a very long time. When she lifted the lid, her jaw dropped at the sight of the legal-sized folders crammed into the box. She spotted her name on one of them. Kelly Young.

Why were there two files from her adoption? A bad feeling settled in the bottom of her stomach and grew as she yanked the folder from the box and opened it to the light. The smell of old dust and mildew scented the pages.

"Caucasian female," she read of her own description in the paperwork, "born to—"

She couldn't see the name and held it up to the harsh light of the bare lightbulb overhead. There had been a name, but it had been blacked out. The father was unknown. It was a California birth certificate.

It was her birth date. Her statistics. Curious, she

asked Ben to reach the records she'd found earlier. When she dug out her real adoption certificate, she held them both up to the light. The little footprints on the documents matched perfectly.

There were two different records. Two different stories of where she'd come from. How could that be? She was born right here in Chestnut Grove, right? Carol and Marcus Young, those were her parents. Which was the truth?

"You look pretty upset." Ben commented from the chair next to her desk, steaming coffee cup in hand. "Is there something I can help you with? I can lift, push, fix, demolish or nail anything you want. But something tells me that's not the kind of help you need right now."

"What I need is a friend."

"Well, I'm here." He carried her untouched coffee cup in. "I take it these boxes aren't good news."

"No." She set aside the contradictory birth records. The coffee smelled great and she took a few long sips. "You were adopted, too, right?"

"This agency handled it. That's why I'm a volunteer."

"What if I told you that I found some secret records. Information on me and several people I know, like you, who were adopted through this agency."

"Me?"

She nodded and set the cup aside. "This is important. It's my life. It's yours."

Ben looked shell-shocked. "I'd want to know the truth."

There were so many files. So many children like herself and Ben. "I'm going to find the truth, whatever it costs."

* * * * *

Dear Reader,

Thank you for choosing *For the Twins' Sake*. Meg's struggle touched me very deeply. Hardships happen to all of us—it's a part of living in this world, and sometimes it is so hard to understand adversity's place in the path God has chosen for us. Meg has been betrayed by her husband and feels as if God has abandoned her, too. She feels lost and alone, but when she realizes that her heavenly Father has been walking with her all along, she can finally open her heart to her new husband's steadfast love.

Blessings to you,

Jillian Hart

Rachel Noble gets up-close-and-personal
with her adopted little sister's
handsome paediatrician in
BROUGHT TOGETHER BY BABY
coming only to Love Inspired
in August 2005.
For a sneak preview, please turn the page.
And keep reading for an extra-special bonus!

Chapter One

Rachel pulled out her cell phone, and the stiffened, the call forgotten as a motorcycle pulled up beside her. Its obscene roar drowned out the gentle sounds of the Brahms symphony coming from her car's CD player.

The driver pulled up beside her, and stopped. He straddled the motorcycle, easily holding it up as he waited. He wore a denim jacket, blue jeans and cowboy boots.

She clenched the steering wheel with a white-knuckled grip. She hated motorcycles. If her late fiancé had been driving his tuck that night—

She pushed the futile thoughts aside. That was in the past. Over.

In spite of that, she couldn't seem to avoid giving the man on the motorcycle a quick glance.

He pushed his helmet back and as she caught his eye, a slow smile crept over his mouth, making his eyes crinkle. Wisps of blond hair curled out from the front of his helmet, framing a lean face.

She looked ahead, angry with herself and the flicker of reaction his lazy good looks.

She made the turn leading to her parents' home and the biker roared past her, leaving her frustrated and with the unwelcome memories this complete stranger had evoked.

She ejected the CD, found a radio station that played classic rock and turned up the volume.

As she drove, she focused on the work that she had to do tomorrow. The jobs that needed her attention. Leave the past in the past.

By the time she turned onto the tree-shaded drive leading to her parents' home, she felt back in control again. The evening was going to be just fine.

She steered her car through a narrow opening between two rows of clipped shrubs that surrounded the main house, pulling up in front of a converted four-car garage.

And her heart flopped over.

The motorcycle that had zipped past her now stood parked on the inlaid brick drive in front of the garage, a helmet hanging from the handlebars.

Great.

She took a long slow breath, just as her yoga instructor had taught her. Focused on the now, the present.

She picked up Gracie's gift and walked with careful, deliberate steps up the brick-paved drive to the front door. Maybe the motorcycle belonged to a delivery man. Or one of the maid's boyfriends.

Her parents' visitor was most likely coming later.

As she stepped inside the door, Aleeda, the housekeeper, swept down the square-rigged flying staircase toward her carrying an armful of linens. With her dark hair worn in a French twist, her patrician features and her aloof bearing, Aleeda DeWindt lent an air of class to the plantation her mother and father didn't care about or exercise. Though Rachel's mother, Beatrice, had admonished their housekeeper time and time again to cut loose and relax, Aleeda preferred a basic uniform of black dress, with white cuffs and collar. She insisted on the same for the two full-time maids who kept the large plantation house spotless and shining.

"Well, well. You're back again," she said smiling at Rachel. "Your mother is in the kitchen, concocting…" She shrugged. "Something."

"Thanks for the warning, Aleeda. Do you have any idea what she plans to feed me?"

"They've got company." Aleeda gave her a mysterious smile. "So I think she'll be doing something more traditional for you and their guest." Aleeda gave her a quick nod, and then strode off to the back of the house before Rachel could ask her who it was that had arrived on that dreadful motorcycle.

Rachel caught her reflection in the mirror hanging in the front hall and took a moment to smooth a wayward strand of chestnut hair back from her forehead. All neat and tidy, she thought. The dark lashes fringing her hazel eyes didn't need mascara. Her cheeks were, well, pale. But so be it.

She whisked one hand down her skirt as she walked down the narrow hallway toward the kitchen, brushing away the few wrinkles she had gotten from driving.

Her mother stood at the huge counter that served as an island in the modernized kitchen, her knife flashing as she chopped vegetables. She wore a bright orange, loose woven shirt over a wildly patterned silk T-shirt in bright hues of turquoise, orange, red and gold that accented her short chestnut hair, worn in a spiky style today. The kitchen table, tucked away in a plant-laden nook, was set with her mother's earthenware dishes. Definitely casual.

"Ah. There you are." Beatrice put down her knife and swept around the island, arms spread out, her shirt and matching skirt flowing out behind her. She enveloped her daughter in a warm hug, holding her close. "I'm so glad you came. And right on time." She drew away, cupping Rachel's face in her narrow hands, her hazel eyes traveling over her daughter's face. "You're looking a little pale, my dear. Have you been taking your kelp supplements?"

Rachel lifted her hand in a vague gesture. "I've been busy…" She laid the present for Gracie on the counter.

"Honey, honey, honey." Beatrice shook her head in admonition. "You have to take care of yourself. Your body is a temple of the Holy Spirit. God needs healthy servants to do His work on earth."

Rachel merely smiled. She wasn't going to get into a discussion with her mother over what God needed or didn't need.

For the past eight years she had put God out of her life. Or tried to. Now and again glimpses of Him would come through, but she generally managed to ignore them. She preferred her independence and God required too much and gave too little.

Beatrice slipped her arm around Rachel's shoulders and drew her toward the counter. "Your father and I have a lovely surprise for you. Gracie's paediatrician said he would come and visit us."

"He's here now?"

Beatrice nodded, giving her daughter a sly grin. "I thought you might want to meet him."

A moment of awareness dawned. "Is he the fool on the motorcycle?"

Beatrice frowned and tapped her fingers on her daughter's shoulders. "Rachel Augusta Charlene Noble, you shouldn't use words like that. Especially about some as wonderful as Eli."

Rachel had hoped that adopting not-yet-two-year-old Gracie would have satisfied her mother's deep-rooted desire for grandchildren. Well, this was one romance she was going to nip in the bud. "I'm sorry, Mom, but as far as I'm concerned, anyone who drives a motorcycle isn't firing on all cylinders. *Especially* if he's a paediatrician." Rachel picked a baby carrot from the bowl sitting on the counter and took a bite. "Where's Dad?"

"He and the estimable Dr. Eli are out in the garden with Gracie. I do believe they're coming back now."

Rachel wandered over to the window overlooking the grounds, propping the last of the carrot in her mouth. A tall, narrow-hipped man sauntered alongside her father, the tips of his fingers pushed into the front pockets of his blue jeans, his softly worn shirt flowing over broad shoulders. He reached over and feathered a curl of Gracie's hair back from her face, smiling softly at her. Gracie laughed up at him and snuggled closer to her father.

Rachel couldn't mesh the picture with the one she'd had created of Gracie's Dr. Eli. Until her mother's pronouncement she had always pictured the man her parents spoke so highly of as an older, portly gentleman, not this…cowboy.

Who drove a motorcycle.

And now,
turn the page for a sneak preview of
SUSPICION OF GUILT,
the second book in
THE MAHONEY SISTERS *miniseries*
by Tracy V. Bateman, part of Steeple Hill's
exciting new line, Love Inspired Suspense!
On sale in September 2005
from Steeple Hill Books.

Prologue

The night swirled around her. Black, stabbing darkness conjuring terrible shadows from childhood nightmares. Leaves hovered like a vampire's cape, suffocating. Fear gripped her. Branches tossed in the breeze—razor-sharp fingers ready to slice her to shreds.

Hurry, hurry, hurry.

A low half-growl, half-whine came from the Doberman behind the fence next door. She jerked her head at the sound, heart pounding in her ears like the thrum of a thousand drums.

Shh. "It's okay," she whispered. *Don't give me away. I'm so close to accomplishing my goal.* The dog sat—watching but silent.

Relief flooded her as she turned back to her task. Denni Mahoney, with all of her sweetness and nice…

Shards of rage pierced through her heart at the thought of Denni getting what she wanted. She didn't deserve it. A mastermind of deception. Denni had fooled them all.

The thought made her smile with grim determination.

With a shaky hand she reached for the outside faucet. Hesitated. One twist and the broken pipe would send water rushing inside the house instead of flowing to the ground. The basement would flood.

She grasped the faucet tight and gave it a quick turn. Water spewed.

The Doberman barked.

Her heart rate escalated. She pushed to her feet, gulping down the fear. She crept across the yard. Relief slowly shoved away the terror of night as she found safety.

Chapter One

Shock, disbelief, horror…all vied for first place in Denni Mahoney's chest as she stared at the foot of water standing in her basement. Water. Just…standing there where water was never meant to be. Despair clutched her heart and squeezed the breath from her lungs. She shook her head, pressing her palm to her forehead.

What next?

"We'll get to the bottom of this." Behind her, Detective Reece Corrigan's tone was hard-edged, resolute, but the warmth of his hand on her shoulder evoked a strange sense of comfort.

"You have to admit it definitely could be one of them. Why do you insist that all five of the girls are innocent?"

The warm, comforting fuzzies turned to cold stone. She didn't have to admit any such thing and she was sick of his suspicions being centered on the girls. Anger shoved down the tears clogging her throat, and she shook off his hand.

Standing on the fourth step from the bottom of the

basement stairs, Denni watched a hardback book float across the water covering the concrete floor. *A Tale of Two Cities*. A birthday gift from her mom when she'd turned fifteen. Little by little her memories of Mom were being destroyed. It had been ten years since her death, and only photos provided a clear picture of her face anymore.

Denni grimaced and abruptly turned away, but Reece's body on the step above her blocked her flight up. Even when she sent him her fiercest frown, he didn't budge.

She drew in the subtle scent of his spicy aftershave. Understated appeal. She liked that about him. The guy had to know how he affected women—a muscular physique and a masculinity that intimidated Denni, yet left her wishing he'd stay close.

"Well?" he asked, the tension in his voice replaced by a subtle, low tone that seeped over her like a gentle rain.

She gaped, fighting the warmth creeping to her cheeks. "Well what?" she whispered.

"I'm going to have to question them again. Who should I speak with first this time?"

"Oh, Reece," she said, hearing the fatigue in her tone. She was so tired. So very, very tired. "Leave the girls alone, will you? How can you blame them for a flood?"

Her girls. Troubled, ex-foster-care kids who were too old to stay in the system but too young to be out on their own. As a social worker, she had grown tired of seeing so many of these girls end up on public assistance, their own children placed in foster care, so she'd opened a home.

Only five young women lived with her, but if her experiment panned out, she had commitments from several local churches to help buy two more homes, each housing ten girls. Monday she was supposed to host a luncheon for the liaisons from each of these churches. How could she explain to potential sponsors that the cops suspected her girls of sabotage?

Denni glanced back at the basement, searching for escape from the confrontation that was surely to come. It was either hike down the steps and swim through the murky water or face Reece's rock-solid stubbornness. She sighed, knowing there was only one logical choice. She'd have to face him.

Forcing herself away from the sight of so many of her treasures soaked and more than likely ruined, she braced for the coming conflict a tiresome, constant echo of accusation.

"Admit it," he demanded.

Deliberately, she lifted her gaze and met his. His steely green eyes silently commanding her to accept the possibility.

"I admit only one thing. It looks like someone is trying to sabotage my efforts to make a nice home for these girls." A sigh pushed from her lungs. "What I can't figure out is why."

Detective Corrigan scowled. "That's what I'm here for, and I have to tell you…"

Denni raised her hand to stop his opinion from flying out of his mouth. "What possible motive could any of them have to sabotage their own home? Where would they go?"

Leaving him to mull over that bit of reason, she scraped against his bomber jacket as she maneuvered around him and marched to the top of the stairs. He followed her into the kitchen.

"That's the one thing I can't put my finger on. It doesn't make a lot of sense, but maybe the person we're dealing with here doesn't think along rational lines."

"All my girls are rational," Denni snapped.

His amusement was more than apparent in the upward curve of his lips. "Then I guess they must take after you," he drawled.

Take 2 inspirational love stories FREE!

PLUS get a FREE surprise gift!

Mail to Steeple Hill Reader Service™

In U.S.
3010 Walden Ave.
P.O. Box 1867
Buffalo, NY 14240-1867

In Canada
P.O. Box 609
Fort Erie, Ontario
L2A 5X3

YES! Please send me 2 free Love Inspired® novels and my free surprise gift. After receiving them, if I don't wish to receive anymore, I can return the shipping statement marked cancel. If I don't cancel, I will receive 4 brand-new novels every month, before they're available in stores! Bill me at the low price of $4.24 each in the U.S. and $4.74 each in Canada, plus 25¢ shipping and handling and applicable sales tax, if any*. That's the complete price and a savings of over 10% off the cover prices—quite a bargain! I understand that accepting the books and gift places me under no obligation ever to buy any books. I can always return a shipment and cancel at any time. Even if I never buy another book from Steeple Hill, the 2 free books and the surprise gift are mine to keep forever.

113 IDN DZ9M
313 IDN DZ9N

Name	(PLEASE PRINT)	
Address	Apt. No.	
City	State/Prov.	Zip/Postal Code

Not valid to current Love Inspired® subscribers.

Want to try two free books from another series?
Call 1-800-873-8635 or visit www.morefreebooks.com.

* Terms and prices are subject to change without notice. Sales tax applicable in New York. Canadian residents will be charged applicable provincial taxes and GST. All orders subject to approval. Offer limited to one per household.

® are registered trademarks owned and used by the trademark owner and or its licensee.

INTLI04R   ©2004 Steeple Hill